"Tell me – talk to me," Barrett pressed urgently

"I can help you, Caroline."

"No," she denied. "You can't help. Nobody can help. This is between myself and Lawrence and Sta—" She stopped abruptly, realizing she had almost blurted out Stacy's name. Barrett wasn't stupid. He would push until he found out all the answers, if she was weak enough to drop unconscious clues.

He pounced. "Between you and Lawrence and...who, Caroline?" Then suddenly recalling the conversation he had overheard last night after he had dumped Lawrence in the elevator, he moved in for the kill. "Between you and Lawrence and *Stacy*, Caroline? Is that what you were about to say?"

Caroline's guilty start was an admission in itself.

"Who is Stacy, Caroline? Your daughter? Your sister? Who?"

WELCOME
TO THE WONDERFUL WORLD
OF *Harlequin Romances*

Interesting, informative and entertaining,
each Harlequin Romance portrays an appealing
and original love story. With a varied array
of settings, we may lure you on an African safari,
to a quaint Welsh village, or an exotic Riviera
location—anywhere and everywhere that adventurous
men and women fall in love.

As publishers of Harlequin Romances, we're
extremely proud of our books. Since 1949,
Harlequin Enterprises has built its publishing
reputation on the solid base of quality and
originality. Our stories are the most popular
paperback romances sold in North America; every
month, six new titles are released and sold at
nearly every book-selling store in Canada and the
United States.

For a list of all titles currently available,
send your name and address to:

HARLEQUIN READER SERVICE,
(In the U.S.) P.O. Box 52040, Phoenix, AZ 85072-2040
(In Canada) P.O. Box 2800, Postal Station A
5170 Yonge Street, Willowdale, Ont. M2N 5T5

We sincerely hope you enjoy reading
this Harlequin Romance.

Yours truly,

THE PUBLISHERS
Harlequin Romances

Darker Fire

Morgan Patterson

Harlequin Books

TORONTO • NEW YORK • LONDON
AMSTERDAM • PARIS • SYDNEY • HAMBURG
STOCKHOLM • ATHENS • TOKYO • MILAN

Original hardcover edition published in 1984
by Mills & Boon Limited

ISBN 0-373-02667-6

Harlequin Romance first edition January 1985

CHAPTER ONE

RONALD WAXLER's dim brown eyes slid over the girl seated in front of him—one could barely call her a woman—then flicked impassively back to the application on his desk. Where do they come from? he wondered idly. Yes, she had the best qualifications of anyone who had applied. Yes, she spoke all the required languages fluently, and then some. And yes, from the faintly desperate look in her eyes she obviously needed the job.

But giving this child a position working closely with Barrett Rossiter—*the* Barrett Rossiter, he amended mentally in a suitably awed tone—would be like a drifting hand to a pack of hungry piranha ... too tempting to resist a nibble. If the gossip in the office was to be believed, the man was a notorious womaniser. Ronald wished he had half the arrogant magnetism that Barrett Rossiter possessed in such disgusting abundance.

Some long-latent streak of protective chivalry turned his mouth down at the corners and added a definite tone of discouragement to his words.

'You realise that Mr Rossiter prefers a man in this position?' he invented wildly.

'No, I wasn't aware of that,' Caroline Forsythe responded pleasantly, no trace of her inner fear showing on her beautiful, calm face. 'That sounds dangerously like sexual discrimination——' she was interrupted by a panicked gobbling noise from Mr Waxler, '—something I'm sure no one can *afford* to subscribe to,' she stressed sweetly.

That innocent exterior was deceptive, Mr Waxler was beginning to discover, as many before him had. This little female could take care of herself, after all. He was

5

sorely tempted to hire her just to see her squash Barrett
Rossiter with one sweet, quelling sentence. He shook his
head visibly. Fantasy, pure fantasy. No one—no one—
had ever 'squashed' Barrett Rossiter. In fact, it worked
just opposite, and Ronald Waxler did not want to be
responsible for the inevitable outcome of any confrontation between Rossiter and this woman. He just
couldn't stand to see women broken and bleeding at
Barrett Rossiter's feet. Metaphorically speaking, of
course. Rossiter would never actually hit a woman—he
had much more subtle ways of destroying them.

Still, if the boss saw her application and realised that
Caroline Forsythe was the most qualified for the job, he
would want to know the reason why she had not been
hired, Ronald realised glumly. One thing Barrett
Rossiter had never been accused of was discrimination.
He didn't care whether an employee was young or old,
male or female, white, black, yellow, red, or purple, as
long as that employee performed his duties capably and
efficiently. Ronald didn't feel up to another lashing
from Rossiter's tongue. He was still smarting from the
last time.

His gaze drifted to the wide gold wedding band
encircling the ring finger of Caroline's left hand. He
seemed to clutch at it like a lifeline.

'At least you're married,' he muttered beneath his
breath, seeming, to Caroline, to take some strange
comfort in the thought.

Caroline opened her mouth to correct him, then
snapped it shut tightly. If Ronald Waxler felt consoled
by the idea that she was married, let him. It didn't
matter to her what he thought, what anyone thought. If
it made her seem in any way more suitable for the
position—in Ronald Waxler's eyes or in Barrett
Rossiter's—then she felt perfectly justified in encouraging the small misconception.

Lies did not come easily to her, but this . . . this was
for a good cause. And it was something she should
never have had to lie about anyway! she told herself

angrily. Barrett Rossiter had no right to include the possession of a husband as a necessary qualification for the job.

She needed this job, needed it desperately. It was her only chance of getting Stacy away from Lawrence. Jobs that demanded her special skills as both interpreter and secretary were few and far between, and Caroline was determined that this one would be hers. So much depended on it.

Firstly, and more importantly, the position paid extremely well. That was a necessity if she was going to support both Stacy and herself. And probably Lawrence, too, she thought resignedly. But even that would be worth it if she got custody of Stacy.

Secondly, the location was right. Stacy would have to change schools, but she would still be close enough to see her friends occasionally. Stacy certainly did not need any more upheaval in her young life.

And finally, this was the job Caroline had dreamed about as she struggled through the years of her training, refusing help from Lawrence during the first, kind years, instinctively knowing that some day it would be withdrawn. She had put herself through college, holding down two and even three jobs to provide for tuition, fees, and books. But she had done what she set out to do, and now she had a chance at the job she had always wanted. The position called for someone who spoke French, Spanish, Arabic and Japanese with a fair degree of fluency, possesed the typing and shorthand skills of a top executive secretary, and was not afraid to work. Barrett Rossiter demanded much from his employees, but even more from himself. No doubt that was how he had come from nowhere, with nothing, and built the Rossiter Organisation, starting at the tender age of twenty with one not-so-healthy business and proceeding from there. Thirteen years later, it was only one of dozens of companies under the Organisation's corporate umbrella. The Rossiter Organisation was a curiosity in today's business world, the exception rather than the rule, Caroline knew. It was one of the few multi-national conglomerates that still had the money and skills to expand, and successfully, at that.

Caroline knew nothing about Barrett Rossiter himself. His picture, his personal affairs never hit the gossip columns. His private life remained exactly that— private, and he guarded it with a fierce intensity that defined intrusion. Nothing was known about his home, his friends, or his women—except that he kept all three. No one would ever find anything in his personal affairs to hold over him in his business ones.

Mr Waxler could have—and probably would have— told her about the rumours that ran rampant through the company headquarters, had Caroline shown one speck of interest. She did not.

She was not interested in her prospective employer's private life. It was none of her business what he did with his time, and she had no intention of intruding in an area of someone else's life when she would not allow the intrusion into her own. She respected other's privacy, and she expected them to accord her the same respect.

'Is there anything else, Mr Waxler?' she asked repressively, seeing the eager light in his eyes that indicated a string of indiscretions hovering on the tip of his tongue.

'No, no, that's quite all, Mrs Forsythe,' Ronald Waxler replied petulantly, cheated out of his gossip. 'You will receive a letter in a week or so,' he continued briskly, rising to his feet belatedly as Caroline was pulling on her coat.

'Fine. I'll——' Her polite words of departure were cut short by the forceful opening thrust of the office door, no knock preceding it.

Impatient strides carried a tall, broad-shouldered man into the room, his eyes fixed on the document in his hand. His hard, angular face was twisted with anger.

'Ron, you have to find——' The furious exclamation was halted abruptly as the intruder raised smoke-grey eyes and met Caroline's sparkling green ones across the width of the room.

The anger died quickly from the stormy depths, turning them a speculative, dove-soft grey. A long, measuring, completely masculine assessment followed, taking in Caroline's long red-gold hair, the almond-shaped jewel eyes, widely-spaced and furious, and the delicate perfection of her classic nose. His eyes settled fractionally on the sweet curve of her mouth before moving on to the firm, determined chin and the warm creamy glow of her skin. He skimmed lightly over her body, lingering appreciatively on the slender curves revealed beneath the severe cut of her businesslike suit.

The entire survey took less than twenty seconds, but by the time his eyes had moved back to her face, Caroline was trembling with a reaction she could not identify. It was as if this man had run his hands over her instead of his eyes, and come away knowing every secret part of her intimately. She hated the sensation, and she steeled herself to hate the man who had aroused it, knowing by some primitive instinct that this would be her only protection.

Her jade eyes studied him in turn, clinically dissecting every small part that added up to the intimidatingly masculine whole. He was tall, six foot three or four, she decided, with shoulders to match. His body was long and taut, an iron strength shouting from beneath the expensively tailored suit that did little to hide the back-alley toughness that lurked beneath the civilised veneer. Caroline would be willing to bet that he had been born in some dark back alley with an instinctive knowledge of protection and destruction. The knowledge lay buried in those expressive grey eyes, and it frightened her slightly. His hair was thick and dark, a slight, uncontrollable wave defying severe styling. It was simply brushed impatiently back from the broad, lined forehead and well marked brows. Slashing dimples would carve themselves into the taut skin of his cheeks when he smiled, she was sure. And his mouth ...

Caroline's eyes skittered away from its length uneasily, unnerved by the intriguing mixture of strength and sensuality that lurked there.

She had never in her twenty-three years met a man who affected her so deeply, and now was not the time for it to happen. She had to think of Stacy now, before herself.

Her mouth firmed, and she turned her rage and frustration to the man in front of her, denying the other emotions he had aroused.

He had just walked in as if—as if he owned the place, interrupting her in possibly the most important interview in her life, Caroline seethed silently, deliberately fuelling her anger. Then, then when he finally realises what a rude mistake he's made, he simply stands there and—and strips me with his eyes, apparently having nothing more productive to do with his time!

Caroline knew reasonably that her reaction was out of all proportion to the crime, but there was something about this man's strongly muscled body and the wicked humour glinting in his eyes that immediately, unreasonably infuriated her. Had it been possible, smoke would, at that very moment, be seeping from her ears. And he was enjoying it! she fumed.

The stranger eyed her lazily, one eyebrow shooting up mockingly as he witnessed the clenching of Caroline's small fists.

'I'm sorry, Ron,' he apologised slowly, not sounding in the least bit as though he were. His eyes never left Caroline's flushed face, so he didn't see Ronald Waxler shifting uncomfortably behind his desk. Ronald Waxler hated being called 'Ron'; it made him feel like an adolescent. Yet he could never bring himself to object when Barrett Rossiter trotted out the ridiculous name with such cordial charm. No one ever shortened Rossiter's name, Ronald thought viciously. But then what would they call him?

Caroline, at that moment, had a few suggestions

about what to call the man in front of her, none of them polite.

'I didn't realise you were with someone ...' he paused deliberately, giving either of them a chance to make introductions. Both remained obstinately silent. 'I'll go——'

'There's no need,' Caroline interrupted coldly, her eyes freezing him in the doorway as he prepared to leave.' I was just about to leave. Mr Waxler,' she finally tore her eyes away from the compelling grey ones and turned abruptly to Ronald Waxler, who stood helplessly behind his desk, 'I'll look forward to hearing from you.'

She gathered up her bag and stiffly crossed the room, stopping as she came within inches of the stranger's solid wall of a chest.

'Would you please move?' she demanded haughtily, her tone chill.

'Where would you like me to move to?' the man enquired solicitously, his eyes intimately suggesting—your place?

Alaska! she thought wildly. Away from me. You're dangerous. I can see it in your eyes, and your mouth ...

'Out of the doorway will be fine,' she told him witheringly, her eyes glittering like green ice.

'But you'll leave if I move,' he pointed out mock-gravely.

'I'll leave if you don't,' she shot back tightly.

'Planning to crawl out between my legs, are you?' he enquired with a wide grin, obviously amused by the mental image the words evoked.

'Hardly,' she ground out between clenched teeth. 'I'm planning to walk over you!'

Across the room, Ronald Waxler choked incredulously, but neither of them heard, too involved in their own battle.

The man studied her slender five-foot-six frame from the lofty superiority of his additional nine inches. His grin widened still more, showing beautiful square white teeth.

He probably does toothpaste commercials in his spare time, Caroline decided nastily, the idea of walking over him becoming more appealing by the moment.

A deep, amused laugh rumbled forth, as though he had read her thoughts. Her ears pricked in unwilling pleasure as the rough sound reached her.

'I think I'd better move,' the man agreed solemnly. 'This suit costs a fortune to clean, and I'm afraid your ungainly size fives would just never come out.' There was amused, fascinated mockery underlining each word. With that, he stepped ostentatiously out of the doorway, waving her to the now unobstructed hall.

'Run away, Red,' he dismissed casually, not missing the flare of anger that lit her eyes at the nickname. 'We'll play another day.'

And that, Caroline considered soberly, sounded dangerously like a threat. Not if I see you first, you—you moving wall! she told him silently, stepping forward with a disdainfully tilted head. She thought it better to maintain a dignified silence with Mr Waxler present and eagerly taking in the whole scene, and probably preparing to relay it to everyone who would listen.

Unfortunately, because her nose was firmly in the air, Caroline did not see the tip of a shiny black expensive shoe resting inconspicuously in her path. Her toe caught on it, and she lurched forward wildly, her arms flailing as she tired to find something to grab on to to regain her balance.

Steel arms caught her mid-air, pulling her forcefully to a rock-hard chest and holding her there firmly. Warm breath tickled at her temple as the man moved his hand to tuck her shining head into his shoulder.

Caroline pushed strongly at the muscled chest, managing to wedge an extremely small slice of space between herself and the warm body pressed so intimately against her own.

She glared furiously into disturbingly grey eyes, shaking as she witnessed the impure intent written there. His black head dipped slowly, his eyes holding her hypnotically.

'Don't you dare!' she hissed warningly, as his lips hovered threateningly above hers. The downward motion halted, and Caroline took the opportunity to wrench herself from his arms.

'You tripped me deliberately!' she accused in disgust, rubbing one hand almost unconsciously over the lips he had so nearly taken.

His eyes, a deep velvet grey now, widened in amusement.

'Why in the world would I want to trip you?' he demanded innocently. 'I would only have to catch you. And I hate holding beautiful sexy redheads in my arms. It makes me all—weak,' he shuddered facetiously, his eyes laughing at her.

'Ooooh!' she seethed. 'You're a—a——'

'Yes?' he prompted politely, interestedly. 'A—a——?'

'I wouldn't lower myself to your level by saying it,' she informed him loftily, triumphantly.

'But it's okay if you think it, hmm?' he murmured smoothly, nodding his dark head in sage understanding.

'No! That's not——' the mockery in his eyes stemmed the outraged flow of her words. 'Goodbye!' she snapped sharply, turning on her heel and stalking regally from the room, her spine stiff.

Oh, my God, she thought sickly as she traversed the hall, her steps grinding punishingly into the thick pile carpet, wishing it was that—that man's mocking face. That Mr Waxler had witnessed that inexcusable explosion of temper! And especially after she had spent a long, painstaking hour convincing him how cool and unflappable she was! She would never get the job now, and all because of that nasty man. It was all his fault. She unfairly heaped the blame squarely on his smooth black head. As she waited for the elevator to arrive, Caroline passed two enjoyable minutes devising suitably gruesome fates for the tall, bad-tempered stranger. After much grim reflection, she settled on boiling him in oil. Feeling marginally better, the image firmly implanted in her angry mind, she stepped into the elevator.

Back in Ronald Waxler's office, the much maligned man in question straightened from his vantage point in the doorway as the elevator doors closed on the bristling woman. He sighed, then turned enquiringly towards the desk.

'And who,' he demanded, his mouth curling with unholy amusement, 'was that?'

'Caroline Forsythe,' Ronald supplied weakly, feeling drained by the interchange he had just witnessed. 'She was interviewing for the interpreter/secretary position. But I suppose now . . .' he continued more cheerfully, 'there's no chance you'd want——'

'Is she qualified?' Barrett demanded sharply, almost not caring if she were or not, his eyes still gleaming with enjoyment.

'Well, yes,' Ronald conceded, 'but——'

'Hire her.'

'But . . . she's too young,' Ronald protested feebly.

'How young?' Barrett questioned curtly.

'Twenty-three.'

'That's not too young,' Barrett denied in cynical amusement.

'I'll bet!' Waxler muttered beneath his breath, his imagination supplying situations in a way his wife would never have believed.

Steely eyes turned on him dangerously. 'What did you say?'

'I—I'm not finished interviewing,' Ronald back-pedalled hurriedly, deeming it imprudent to repeat himself. He was already resigned to the inevitable outcome of this conversation—Barrett Rossiter had not got where he was today by taking no for an answer—but he felt it necessary to offer a token protest.

'I don't give a damn. Hire her,' Barrett repeated, his words too soft, his tone too gentle.

Ronald gulped audibly. 'Yes, Mr Rossiter,' he agreed.

'Good,' Barrett nodded in satisfaction, eyeing Ronald Waxler pityingly. The man was a worm, an obsequious little worm who sucked up to him every chance he got. Barrett had told him many times to call him by his first name, preferring a casual relationship with his employees, but Waxler steadfastly resisted. Barrett was no fool. He had read all the hidden resentment seething in Ronald Waxler, and accepted it. It was something he had run into more than once over the years, as the Organisation grew.

Still, he thought triumphantly, he had arrived at Waxler's office in time to see Caroline Forsythe and ensure that she was hired. Barrett strolled out of the office, whistling.

The little worm slouched unhappily behind his desk.

'He didn't even tell me why he came barging in here in the first place,' Ronald muttered glumly.

Barrett Rossiter whistled all the way back to his penthouse office suite. He didn't know why he was whistling. He didn't know why he felt so suddenly happy. And he didn't know why he had instructed Ronald Waxler to hire one Miss Caroline Forsythe. Well, he amended mentally, maybe he did know why he had done that. She was sure as hell beautiful, and she had stood up to him. No one—especially the women in his life—stood up to him the way she had.

Yes, he decided, shifting comfortably in the leather chair behind his beautiful oak desk, that was why he had hired Caroline Forsythe. He enjoyed the change and the challenge of her. But there was something more, something just beyond his grasp. He closed his eyes, the better to concentrate, his long body suddenly stiffening as the realisation hit him.

Dear God, he *wanted* her.

For years he had played the game, automatically, his moves mechanical, emotionless in a way. In the early days, even before his formidable success in building the Rossiter empire, there had still been women—rich women, beautiful women drawn by Barrett's hard confidence and steely eyes. And he had watched, those steely eyes shadowed with cynicism as the women multiplied with the size of his bank account. His wealth an added attraction, and he never deluded himself about that. So he had taken what was offered, discreetly, selectively choosing only those who knew the score and wanted nothing more than physical pleasure and pretty gifts. Barrett knew, with a nagging sense of emptiness, that there was nothing more he wanted to give them. Yes, his body had responded to practised caresses, his senses had stirred to hungry demands, but his mind, his emotions, his soul had remained his own, untouched by the need to possess and be possessed.

And now for the first time in his life he had come face to face with a need so intense, so completely overwhelming, that it left him shaking beneath its hungry burden.

He wanted Caroline Forsythe, wanted her warmth and her softness, her spirit and her light. He wanted to hold her, caress her, make her flame beneath his touch. The thought closed his stunned grey eyes as the image imprinted itself in his mind and tantalised his senses.

Barrett Rossiter had stopped whistling.

Caroline shuddered thankfully as she reached the old, three-storey house where her apartment was located. The house, a relic from Denver's past, had long since been divided into separate flats. It was ugly, especially in the dull, dreary Colorado winter, its shuttered windows staring bleakly on the street. The plumbing was erratic—part of the original design, Caroline was sure—the heating system sporadic, and the interior a uniform dirty grey. But part of it belonged to her, she thought possessively. And besides, it was all she could afford. And that was the reality, she acknowledged flatly.

She hauled herself heavily up the two flights of stairs that led to her apartment. Somewhere along the line an elevator had been installed in the sprawling house, but

Caroline was too impatient to wait for its arrival. It took days to arrive, preferring, temperamentally, to stop on every floor and in between, too, as though to assure itself that no timid soul was waiting, too shy to press the call button. Caroline's landlady thought the eccentric, ancient elevator 'cute'. Caroline, at that moment, could have supplied a much more fitting adjective.

Walking down the hallway to her apartment, she let her mind drift once more over the disastrous events of that afternoon.

She had presented herself to Mr Waxler so hopefully, knowing that she was qualified and determined that she would get the job. Stacy's whole future depended on it.

Reaching her apartment door, she fitted the key in the lock and pushed forward into the room, assessing the slightly shabby neatness of the living room with dull eyes. She had been lucky enough to get what had once been the master bedroom. It was a huge room, complete with large windows and a fireplace, that had been cheaply sectioned off to form a self-sufficient flat.

Caroline dropped defeatedly into the nearest chair, her eyes moving despairingly around the uninspired room. She had had such high hopes when she had rented this place, seeing Stacy and herself happily together at last. But that had depended on this job, and she had destroyed all chance of being hired now. If only she had not lost her temper with that obnoxious stranger, if only she had remained cool, aloof from those amused grey eyes, if only she had ignored that blatantly masculine assessment. If only . . .

If only she were the kind of person who could control her own impulsive temper, she admitted wryly. God knew, after seven years of living with Lawrence it was a minor miracle that it had not been knocked out of her by now.

If Lawrence were here right now, she thought bitterly, he would be very, very happy.

She cringed, seeming to shrink into the depths of the

tattered armchair as the memories crowded into her mind, and the whole hurtful story played itself out one more time . . .

They had been such a happy family. Caroline, at the age of fifteen, had just begun to understand the very special love her parents shared. Robert and Marie had been married seventeen years, and still held hands as they sat on the front porch swing and exchanged secret, loving smiles over Caroline's head.

When Stacy had been born—at some risk because Marie was then thirty-six—her parents had been ecstatic, and Caroline, if possible, more so. Stacy had been no 'surprise package' sprung on them and disturbing the even tenor of their lives. They had so much love between them, and so much more to give, and Caroline and her parents acknowledged the need to share that love. They had considered adopting, but Marie had desperately wanted to bear Robert's second child, and her father, Caroline was sure, was secretly aching to see his wife heavy with child, despite his weak protests.

Robert had been almost fanatical about the care Marie took during her pregnancy, begging her not to stand too long, not to eat too much, not to work too hard. The list was endless. Marie had listened to his directives with loving indulgence and proceeded to do exactly as she wanted.

The pregnancy was difficult from the start. Twice in the first twelve weeks, Marie had almost miscarried. The delivery drained her completely. Yet when she had finally held her new daughter in her arms she had become revitalised, glowing with a wondrous excitement and pride. When her father had held Stacy for the first time, Caroline remembered sadly, he had hugged her so tightly that the baby had begun to cry in protest, and Robert had soothed her gently, somehow managing to look shamefaced and blissful at the same time.

Caroline had been lost from the moment Stacy had peered up at her with deep, unfocused eyes. Their family circle had expanded to include one tiny life, and the bonds had been forged even stronger with the love she brought.

And then, without warning, Robert Forsythe had suffered a massive heart attack and died, leaving them alone to build a world without the protective shadow of his love and support.

Marie crumbled completely on the death of her husband. Without him she became a lifeless shell, empty and hollow. She went on living only for the sake of her children. Caroline tried to comfort her, but Marie only looked at her with a vacant smile and shook her head sadly. It was as if she had died with her husband, yet her body remained bound to the physical world. Fearfully, Caroline watched her mother slip away from them.

Even Stacy, at six months old, had felt the loss. Marie could only study the fretful baby bewilderedly, unable to supply her needs. It fell to Caroline, during those first awful, empty months, to care for her sister. Love and loneliness made it easy.

They lived for weeks in a kind of limbo, drifting aimlessly. The insurance money they had received upon Robert's death had shielded them to some extent from the harsh reality of their situation, but Caroline, even at fifteen, knew the money wouldn't last for ever. She had offered to leave school and find a job, but Marie had flatly refused.

Marie was not a weak woman, but her entire life had been spent in the warm protection of Robert's love. She knew no skills, and, alone, was too apathetic to make the effort.

And then came Lawrence Redden.

He showed up at their front door one day two months after Robert's funeral. He was an old war buddy, he claimed, paying a friendly visit when he found himself in town. A strangely avid expression twisted his features as Marie stonily related the fact of Robert's death. It was that expression, as briefly it had crossed his face, that put Caroline on her guard.

Lawrence Redden was a fast talker, and gradually Marie came to rely on him more and more as he took over the running of their lives. Six months after Robert's death, he had asked Marie to marry him, and Marie, her heart forever buried with Robert, had accepted. Caroline had argued violently against the proposed marriage, hating the way Lawrence's mouth twisted every time Robert's name was mentioned, but her mother refused to listen to any of her protestations, listlessly pointing out that Stacy needed a father even if Caroline did not. Caroline could not sway her.

On the night before her wedding, Marie removed Robert's wedding band from her finger and gave it to Caroline.

'Wear it for me, Caro,' she begged, her eyes anguished. 'I can't let him go completely.' She sounded like a frightened child, Caroline thought sadly, slipping the band on her own ring finger, the continuation of her parents' vows. The ring was never removed from her finger. Sometimes Marie's eyes would rest on it, hungry and sad. Lawrence ignored its existence with a bitter intensity that spoke far louder than words. To Caroline, it was the symbolic weight of dreams that had died.

For the first three or four years, things had gone remarkably well. Lawrence treated them patiently, providing the necessities and lavishing attention on Marie. If she was never touched by any of it, if she sometimes seemed to be lost in her memories, Lawrence carefully ignored it. He was trying desperately to win her love. But he was fighting to steal something Marie could not give. All her love, all of herself lay buried with Robert.

As time passed, Lawrence's love turned bitter and tortured. Finally he realised that Marie had nothing to give him, that Robert had taken it all, and he struck out in pain and anger.

His cruelties became more refined as the months passed, and his hatred grew harder. He denied Marie the right to visit Robert's grave as she did every

Sunday, and when she defied him, he retaliated by threatening Caroline with a severe beating. It was the only weapon he had against the bleak wall of Marie's indifference, for she had long ago ceased to care about herself. Marie never again visited the grave of her dead husband.

Over the next year Lawrence used his weapon ruthlessly, and each time Marie slipped further and further away. The very tactics he used to bind her to him pushed her away. He hit out with the confused violence of a wounded animal.

In the final months of her marriage, Marie became a shadow of herself. She seldom left the house, seeming unable to rise from her bed. At the beginning of her illness the family doctor, Edward Hilton, had come regularly, demanding each time that Marie be hospitalised. Lawrence rejected the idea and finally refused to let Dr Hilton see Marie again, his face hard and furious. Caroline never knew the reason behind this action. She was frantic, each day her mother retreated further away.

Finally, unable to watch any longer, she called Edward Hilton, and he had come one final time. Caroline had ensured that he came at a time when Lawrence would be out of the house—down at the corner bar where he now spent most of his time.

Edward pleaded with Marie to let him take her away from Lawrence, some place where she and the girls could start a whole new life together and Lawrence would never find them.

'I'll help you, Marie,' he promised urgently. 'I'll help you and the girls in any way you'll let me, I promise you. Please, come with me now.'

Marie shook her head, regarding Edward as though he were a particularly backward child who had not been able to grasp the simplest of teachings.

'No, Edward,' she told him slowly, enunciating each word distinctly. 'I will not go away. I do not want to start a new life.'

'What about the girls?' Edward persisted. 'What are they going to do after——?' he broke off, a silent understanding hanging heavily in the air between them, and Caroline shivered fearfully.

'Caroline is twenty-two now. She only stays because of me. She graduates this month. She'll be free, self-sufficient——' here Marie broke off, her mouth twisted in an unbelievably bitter smile. 'She'll take care of Stacy. She's been more of a mother to her than I have . . .'

'But you have to try, Marie,' Edward urged gently. 'You have to try!'

'No,' Marie answered with calm certainty, 'I don't. Edward, I'm so tired. There's nothing more to say. I want to sleep now.' Her eyelids fluttered down, and within minutes she was asleep.

Edward stayed long after she had fallen asleep, holding her frail hand. After long, silent minutes, he eased himself from her bedside and walked slowly away, suddenly seeming stiff and old.

Two weeks later, on a breezy blue August day, Caroline returned from her morning lectures at the university to find Stacy sitting alone on the front porch of the tiny, ramshackle old house they had lived in since their mother had married Lawrence six years before. Stacy's hands—grubby, as usual—cupped her face dejectedly.

'Hi, munchkin,' Caroline greeted affectionately. 'What are you doing?'

'Nothin',' Stacy muttered in reply. 'I wanted to see Mom, we were going to play a game—she promised me last night. But Lawrence said to get out of the room and stay away from her.' Stacy's tone was hurt. She had never called Lawrence 'Dad', even though she remembered nothing of her own father who had died when she was only six months old. 'She's my mom,' Stacy wailed. 'Why can't I see her, Carly?'

Caroline smiled at the use of the nickname and held her hand out to her little sister. 'Well, let's go and see how Mom feels, okay?'

She was furious. There was no way she would let Lawrence play his sadistic games with Stacy. So far they had been confined solely to Caroline. Stacy was not going to be hurt; she was too young to fight back.

Caroline thought she would never forget the silence of her mother's room, or the stillness of her body as she viewed her mother's bed from the doorway. Lawrence stood near by, staring blankly at one wall, his back to the still form on the bed.

Caroline released Stacy's hand, taking one stumbling, numb step towards the bed, before Stacy's voice halted her.

'Ask her if we can play, okay, Carly?' she whispered pleadingly, unconsciously subdued by the deathly silence of the room.

Caroline turned and dropped to her knees beside Stacy's skinny little body, placing gentle hands on either side of her ribcage and shielding her from the sight of their mother.

'Why don't you go out on the porch, honey,' she instructed carefully, praying that Stacy could not feel the trembling of her hands. 'I'll—I'll talk to Mom alone, okay?'

'Okay,' Stacy agreed reluctantly, shooting an un-comprehending look at Lawrence's stiff back before skipping quickly from the room.

Lawrence had not moved a muscle during the entire episode, his big body rigid, his eyes fixed blindly on the wall. Caroline remained where she was, crouched on her knees, too cold, too frightened to rise to her feet. The dark silence filled every corner of the room, every corner of Caroline's mind as she knelt there locked in a stony tableau with Lawrence and the lifeless form that was her mother.

Slowly, awkwardly, she broke out of her frozen stillness, coming to her feet and taking dragging, reluctant steps to her mother's bedside.

Marie lay still and silent in the bed, her skin white. Caroline, with one small part of her mind that was still capable of functioning, registered the expression of blissful peace that had settled on her worry-lined face— a worn soldier who had at last found refuge.

She was dead. Caroline knew it—had known it from the second she had stood in the doorway and registered the unearthly silence of the room.

'Mom——' Caroline drew a ragged breath. 'Mom is dead, isn't she?' she demanded confirmation from Lawrence harshly.

Her words cracked his stillness like a hammer through glass, and he turned to her, staring with empty, indifferent eyes, not speaking.

She tore her eyes away and knelt beside her mother's bed. Silent tears raced heedlessly down her ashen cheeks. She took one cold, lifeless hand in hers and raised it to her face, pressing feverish lips to the back. Glimmering tears landed unnoticed, shining as brightly as diamonds on the pale skin where they fell. She rubbed the chill skin vigorously between her own, desperately trying to instil some kind of warmth, achingly seeking some kind of comfort.

Marie did not move, no words of reassurance spilled from her whitened lips.

Caroline began to trace Marie's still face with hungry fingers, playing with the mask that rested there. Her eyes scanned her mother's face wildly for some sign of life.

'You can't leave us,' she whispered in quiet despair, the mask blurred now through the heavy film of tears filling her jade eyes. 'Please don't leave us,' she begged hopelessly. 'We need you, we love you——'

Violent hands dragged her to her feet, throwing her away from her mother's side.

'Leave her,' Lawrence snarled, his eyes wild with emotion. 'She's gone! Lost to you as she was lost to me all these years . . .' The words were thick with bitter satisfaction.

'Why?' Caroline moaned pitifully, deaf to his words as she stood lost in her grief. 'Why?'

'She's with your father now!' Lawrence spat the words out as if their taste sickened him, his face filled with a harsh light. 'She's with your father now,' he repeated savagely, as though to punish himself, his eyes raging uncontrollably.

Caroline glared at him with an instinctive bitter hatred that would no longer be suppressed. 'You did it,' she accused hoarsely, her heart twisting with pain. 'You killed her! You hated her, you hurt her every time you touched her, every time you looked at her——'

A heavy flattened palm made burning contact with Caroline's cheek, the sharp report echoing off the walls as the force of the blow snapped her head back violently.

'You'll learn, little girl,' Lawrence snarled in stormy satisfaction, reading the pain in her frightened eyes. 'You'll learn that's what love is all about!' His mouth twisted spasmodically, his eyes burning with the dark, hot emptiness of a man lost in a desert. He turned slowly, and left the room with painful, stumbling steps.

Caroline, through the tears and the pain and the terrible chill of death, saw only the stillness of her mother's body.

CHAPTER TWO

CAROLINE almost didn't bother to answer the door when the knock sounded. She sat, dejected and exhausted, in a hard armchair. She had been up at dawn, searching the Help Wanted section of the early morning paper, circling job possibilities, meagre as they were, and marking time until nine when she could begin the tedious calls to set up appointments. By ten-thirty she had left the apartment, armed with a list of interviews that she had scheduled through early evening. In her hand she clutched a bus schedule. Her six-year-old Toyota she kept garaged, in an attempt to use it only when absolutely necessary, and thereby save gas and money. Thank goodness Denver's bus service was efficiently organised!

It was a hopeless, frustrating week. Either she was 'over-qualified' for the jobs available, or they didn't pay enough. Caroline had reached the point where she was willing to accept a low-paying position, and supplement her income with a part-time job after hours. Her savings were running dangerously low and she was getting desperate. If only she had known that all those years of scrimping and saving, balancing a full load of classes and two and even three jobs were going to push her out of the job market, Caroline thought ironically, she wouldn't have bothered. After a long frustrating day of rejections, she had almost begun to wonder why she was bothering now.

Still, when the light rap on the door reached her, she somehow dragged herself from the chair and crossed to the door.

A jolly-faced mailman stood patiently in the hallway, a legal-sized envelope in his hand.

'Got a certified letter here,' he told her cheerfully. 'Need a signature.'

'You must have the wrong apartment——' Caroline began dispiritedly. None of the people who usually wrote to her even knew her new address, and she certainly couldn't think of anyone who would be sending her certified mail.

'Caroline Forsythe?'

She blinked. 'Yes.'

'Then I got the right apartment,' he said in satisfaction, thrusting a clipboard at her. 'Sign?'

She scribbled her name, handed the clipboard back, and had a letter pushed into her hands to replace it.

With a succinct ''bye,' the mailman turned and moved down the hall.

''Bye,' Caroline murmured to the empty air, shutting the door absently.

She studied the letter thoughtfully as she walked back to the armchair and sank into it. Rossiter Organisation—Personnel Department, the return address read clearly.

Her shoulders slumped wearily. A rejection letter. Polite, she was sure. Something along the lines of 'thanks for your application, but no, thanks.' It was probably a form letter, she depressed herself further, without her name even. 'Dear Applicant,' most likely.

Ripping the envelope open uninterestedly, she pulled the letter free.

'Dear Mrs Forsythe,' she read incredulously, 'We are very happy and honoured to offer you the position of Interpreter/Executive Secretary for which you applied. Your qualifications and skills will be a most welcome addition to our company.'

The letter went on to discuss hours and salary—which was even more generous than she had dared hope—and ended with the proposed starting date and a phone number to call in order to notify the personnel department of 'her much hoped-for acceptance of the position.' It was signed, in a fussy, prissy hand, Ronald Waxler.

A disbelieving sigh escaped Caroline's lips.

She had got the job. In spite of everything, she had got the job. Her lips firmed. Now she would get Stacy.

Caroline reached the office much too early on her first day. The guard watched her oddly as she crossed the lobby to his station, glancing surreptitiously at the clock on the wall behind her, his grizzled eyebrows shooting up as he registered the time. An amused understanding lightened his face, however, and a small smile played across his kind mouth as Caroline flashed her shiny new identification card.

'Miss Forsythe,' he greeted her kindly. 'We were told you'd be starting work today. Mr Rossiter is a fine man to work for. I'm sure you'll be happy with us.'

Caroline smiled thankfully at the welcoming speech. She somehow doubted if the guard had ever strung so many words together at one time, and she was sincerely glad that he had made the effort for her.

'Thank you, Mr——' she paused helplessly, realising that she did not know his name.

'Burns,' the guard supplied easily.' 'But call me Sam—everybody does. We don't hold much for formality here.'

'Thank you, Sam,' Caroline spoke lightly. 'And you must call me Caroline. I don't hold much for formality either,' she repeated his words humorously.

Sam nodded decisively, having reached the decision that Caroline Forsythe was a nice woman, and quite good enough to be working with the boss. Ronald Waxler—gossiping old man—had walked around all week with a sour, secretive smile on his prim mouth, as though for once he was hoarding a highly juicy piece of gossip. All he would say was that Caroline Forsythe was a little spitfire, and that she and the boss had had quite a to-do in his office. Waxler reckoned that Miss Forsythe would keep Barrett in line. Sam Burns privately decided that Caroline and Barrett would keep each other on their toes. Again Sam nodded, silently satisfied at the thought.

Caroline relaxed slightly as she witnessed the faint nod. She had no idea exactly what Sam was thinking, but she felt as if she had just been thoroughly and minutely examined, and she breathed a sigh of unconscious relief as an accepting smile curved the line of his mouth. It was important that she keep this job, and the mutual respect and liking between her and her co-workers was the first step.

'Well, Sam, I believe I'd better be getting into the office. I want to check everything out before my real day starts.' She looked around vaguely. The receptionist had not yet arrived, and Caroline realised, chagrined, that she had not the slightest idea of where her office was located. She turned back to Sam helplessly, seeking the guidance of the experienced guard.

'You're sharing Mr Rossiter's office suite,' she was told understandingly. 'It's the penthouse—the door marked "Private".'

'Thank you, Sam,' Caroline breathed gratefully, beginning to feel as if she should make a recording of those three words. Sam Burns had proved extremely helpful, and Caroline didn't doubt that she would be taking advantage of his assistance again before very much time passed.

She strode confidently to the waiting elevators, firmly deciding it was time to at least pretend she knew what she was doing. She stepped in the nearest elevator and pressed the button for the penthouse.

'Good luck,' Sam called sincerely. 'Barrett is wandering around the building, so you'll have a little time to get acquainted before he snaps the whip.' He smiled to show that the remark was meant to be humorous, but Caroline felt a quiver of apprehension clutch at her stomach.

'Thanks, Sam,' she repeated weakly as the doors of the elevator slid silently shut.

She eyed the door marked 'Private' for long seconds before she steeled her nerves sufficiently to twist the knob. She pushed the door inward, standing in the doorway as her eyes studied the room.

It was large, bright and airy, with warm cream walls and an intriguing colour scheme of dark grey and maroon. A long plush sofa rested against one wall, comfortably inviting, and a matching set of chairs flanked it symmetrically. A low mahogany coffee table rested in front of the group, an unusual modern sculpture holding pride of place on its gleaming surface. Caroline knew that no shoes had ever been casually propped on the beautifully crafted table. The office resembled someone's living-room, except for the large desk placed strategically against the back wall, sitting guard over the smooth panelled door that undoubtedly led to the inner sanctums of the penthouse suite.

Crossing to the desk, Caroline scanned its surface judiciously, noting the complicated communications panel and the sleek electronic typewriter doubtfully before checking the desk drawers for supplies. It was extremely well stocked and organised. Whoever had last occupied this desk had been intimidatingly capable.

The thought frightened Caroline momentarily. If she had been so capable, why was she no longer employed here? Was Barrett Rossiter an impossible ogre? No, she squashed the thought firmly. There had been real respect, affection almost, in Sam Burns' voice as he spoke about Barrett Rossiter. And he had used his boss's first name with unconscious ease, after he had given Caroline his silent stamp of approval. No man who could inspire such a reaction in his employees could be all bad.

'So calm down, Caroline,' she muttered beneath her breath, dropping her handbag in a conveniently empty drawer. 'You haven't wandered into cannibal country!'

Slightly reassured, she straightened from the desk and moved to the connecting door between the offices. After knocking tentatively, she pushed the door open and entered the room.

The main room was even larger than her own outer office, intimidatingly efficient and completely masculine. The room was subtly but distinctly divided into various areas. A conversation pit, complete with a low brown couch, several armchairs and conveniently placed tables, comprised the left half of the office. A nearby door led to a personal bathroom/dressing room suite. Caroline lingered only long enough to gape at the gold-plated fixtures and mirrored walls before returning to the main office once more. A highly polished oak meeting table surrounded by high-backed, businesslike chairs sat majestically in its own screened-off room to the right. Barrett Rossiter's desk sat uncompromisingly in the middle of the room, a large bank of windows behind it. Caroline suspected that the location had been chosen not so much for the superb view of Denver the windows afforded as for the shadowing effect the outside light would provide on the person seated behind the desk. While all other occupants of the office would be caught in a glare as bright and relentless as a spotlight, Barrett Rossiter would remain in shadow, his face and his thoughts veiled. A consummate business-man.

Drawn irresistibly to the huge leather chair behind the desk, Caroline cast a guilty glance at the open office door, then, deciding the coast was clear, she dropped into its enveloping depths. It was extraordinarily comfortable, she thought, bounding lightly up and down. And, she discovered gleefully, it spun! A wave of sudden happiness engulfed her. She had a job—a good job. Soon, she promised herself, she would have Stacy. Retreating for one carefree moment to the lost innocence of her childhood, to the years Lawrence had not destroyed, she began to twirl the chair around impulsively.

She was still happily engaged in this pursuit when an amused voice interrupted.

'Well, well,' a mocking, deeply masculine, horribly familiar voice drawled, 'you don't look like Barrett Rossiter!'

Caroline started guiltily, her feet dragging the whirling chair to a halt, bringing her face to face with the man resting indolently against the door frame separating the two offices.

'You!' she exclaimed sharply, eyeing the lean form of the man who had practically cost her this job with furious eyes. 'You—you——!'

The man bowed mockingly from the waist, his eyes glittering with unsuppressed amusement. 'Charming. One of the nicest things you've ever said to me,' he murmured dryly.

'I can think of a whole lot of things I'd like to say to you,' Caroline informed him darkly.

One black brow rose in enquiry. 'Why have you taken such a dislike to me? I haven't done you any harm. And you really can't keep calling me 'you— you——', he went on kindly. 'What would people think? My name is——'

'I don't need to know your name. I can think of plenty of things to call you,' Caroline promised meaningfully. 'You nearly cost me this job! Barging in and making me lose my temper like that——'

'Making you lose your temper?' he interrupted incredulously.

'—after I spent almost an entire morning convincing Mr Waxler how calm and collected I was,' she continued, ignoring his taunt.

'You shouldn't have tried to deceive the poor wor— man.'

'And then, tripping me and making me look like a perfect fool——'

'Oh, not perfect,' he demurred.

'Oooh!' Caroline actually stamped her foot in annoyance. 'I could slap you!'

'I had a horse that did that once,' Barrett observed interestedly.

Caroline was momentarily diverted. 'A horse slapped you?'

'No,' he corrected, tongue in cheek. 'I had a horse who stamped a hoof like that whenever it got angry with me.'

'Then you shouldn't have made him angry,' she told him loftily, her mind busy imagining the satisfaction she would derive from practising a little mayhem upon his person.

'She,' Barrett corrected with a smile. 'And she was angry because I was breaking her in, teaching her to accept my commands ... She's as tame as a kitten now,' he drawled slowly, allowing a smile of dreamy, pleasant remembrance to curl his mouth.

Caroline looked at him much as she would a worm in her salad. 'Fortunately, kittens possess claws and long sharp teeth, and no free animal is truly tamed by an impatient, arrogant hand.'

A grin of unholy amusement spread over his face as he straightened from the doorway and crossed the room to stand within a few short, dangerous inches of her.

'Claws?' he whispered, taking her right hand in his and studying the smooth oval nails painted a bright bold red. 'Maybe,' he conceded, raising her captured hand to his jaw and moving her nails lightly on his skin, causing her to shiver with the sensation. 'As for long sharp teeth,' he shook his head sadly, 'they're reserved for animals of the wild, like panthers and——'

'Wolves?' Caroline supplied with sweet significance.

A hard smile slashed a deep, arresting dimple in Barrett's tanned skin. 'Exactly,' he agreed softly, enjoying the sharp exchange. 'No smart kitten would ever bite the hand that—feeds her.'

Caroline shook herself slightly, deliberately pulling free from the sticky web of sensual innuendo he was weaving. 'I had a cat once,' she told him solemnly, 'who would go for days without eating—if she didn't like what was being offered.'

'Ah, but that's the trick, isn't it?' Barrett nodded wisely. 'Making them like—lust after what's being offered ...'

Caroline tensed at the deliberate use of the word.

'This has gone far enough,' she determined firmly, moving swiftly to the door and holding it open

invitingly. 'Nothing you can say will change the fact
that I almost lost this job because of your—ridiculous
behaviour in Mr Waxler's office.'

'But you didn't lose the job, did you?' he asked.
'You're here, and by all appearances, firmly dug in.
You were probably *lucky* that we—er—ran into each
other,' he told her innocently.

'What does that mean?' Caroline demanded, eyes
narrowed suspiciously.

'Nothing,' he denied, smiling beatifically. 'But
Waxler wasn't going to hire you, you know . . .'

'I know,' she confirmed disgustedly. 'Mr Rossiter
prefers a man in this position,' she mimicked Waxler's
tone perfectly, drawing an unwilling smile to Barrett's
mouth.

'Is that what he told you?'

'Mmm.'

'Well, I can tell you for a fact that Mr Rossiter would
have to be a fool if he preferred anyone but you in this
position, and——' he stopped to smile wolfishly, '—he's
no fool.'

'What did you mean—it was lucky that we ran into
each other?' Caroline's mind clung tenaciously to that
remark.

'Oh, just that there were a lot of applications for
the job and our little encounter made it easier to
remember you from all of the others—for Mr Waxler,
I mean.'

Barrett began to walk towards her with lazy intent as
she stood stiffly, still by the door.

'Look,' she began, licking her bottom lip nervously.
'I don't know who you are or what you want——'

'I could supply the answer to both of those
questions,' he told her whimsically, 'but I somehow
don't think you'd appreciate it . . .'

'But,' Caroline pressed on determinedly, 'Mr Rossiter
is not here, and I'm sure he wouldn't want you messing
around in his office.'

'The way you were, you mean,' he suggested blandly.

'I was not "messing around"!' Caroline denied indignantly. 'I was—well, I was——'

'Messing around,' he finished obligingly. 'Don't you have chairs at home to spin around in?' he questioned curiously.

She thought briefly of her small, sparsely furnished apartment and smiled wryly. 'No,' she answered honestly.

Barrett looked intrigued. 'What do you have at home?'

'Not much,' she acknowledged, her eyes unguarded and sad. She certainly didn't have Stacy.

'You could have me there,' Barrett suggested audaciously. 'Or at my place . . . or on that couch right over there . . .'

Caroline glared at him furiously and turned smartly on her heel, marching into the outer office. 'Get out!' she ordered, motioning invitingly towards the door.

Barrett followed her cheerfully, grinning and unrepentant. 'You don't mean that.'

'Yes, I do,' she shot back. She was not amused. Sam had said that Barrett Rossiter was wandering the building, and she sincerely doubted if he would appreciate entering his office and finding his new secretary/interpreter passing the time of day with this great lolling stranger. 'Please leave.'

He pretended to consider the request. 'Well, I suppose there are a few things I could be doing elsewhere . . .' he began tantalisingly, his mouth dented in amusement as he witnessed the hopeful expression light her face.

'I'm sure,' Caroline agreed dryly.

'On the other hand,' he mused tormentingly, 'there's something that urgently needs doing here.'

'What are you talking about?' she queried, running concerned eyes over the well-ordered suite. 'What needs doing?'

'This.'

He moved so fast Caroline did not have time to ward

him off. She was plucked from her awkward stance in the middle of the office and hauled into the iron band of his arms before she could draw a breath. Then his lips met hers, and she forgot how to breathe, her mind completely taken up with mobile mastery of his touch.

The first touch was tentative, teasing, as his lips brushed against hers lightly, like a diver testing the depths. Caroline's eyes closed instinctively as she awaited his next move. His lips came back to hers, firmer, more slowly as they explored the parted fullness of her lips. He moved from corner to corner with slow enjoyment, tasting, nibbling, teaching, learning. As his mouth moved lightly over her lips, coaxing them apart, his hand moved to rest on the slight curve of her thigh, and Caroline gasped at the dual assault.

'Lady . . .' he breathed against her mouth, his warm breath feathering her skin and caressing her lips, 'whose convent did you escape from?'

She blushed wildly. She did not have much experience, she knew. At the time when her friends had been experimenting with boys and make-up, Caroline had been caring for Stacy and earning money for school. There were times when she had held down two and even three jobs to pay for tuition and books, in addition to carrying a full load of classes. That had left little time for socialising, and Caroline had never felt the void left by this single-minded devotion until this minute, pressed closely against the hard length of this man's body.

She blinked up at him, bewildered. Where did one start?

Barrett's eyes dropped to her parted lips hotly. 'Like that,' he approved with a smothered sigh, lowering his lips once again to hers. 'Exactly like that . . .'

His lips took hers hungrily, intently, stroking arousingly over their trembling fullness and forcing her, with an insistent gentleness, to respond.

Caroline could find no shelter from the storm that raged between them. Her lips met his willingly, and a deep, shuddering stillness encased them in its warmth.

A rising tide of hunger almost submerged her, she pulled away in fear. Hunted, hurried steps put a safe breathing distance between them, as she fearfully studied his passion-dark eyes. She was not so ignorant that she did not know where this was leading and she was not yet ready to tread that path, not with a man who's name she did not know, and in an office her new boss would be entering at any time! She couldn't give in to this wild torrent he had ignited, she couldn't think of herself and her needs now. Stacy was her first priority, and nothing—nothing—was going to divert her attention from her goal of securing custody.

Barrett read the cold flash of sanity in her eyes. 'Caroline,' he began huskily, taking one step towards her, then stopping as she backed away. 'Don't be afraid. Look, I know that it happened too fast, but that was the most——'

'—arrogant, egotistical——' Caroline finished wildly, her eyes bright with fear and bewilderment.

'Don't——' Barrett's words were cut off abruptly as the office door was pushed inward, and a very pretty, very pregnant woman entered.

A flashing smile lit her face as she took in the two people standing in the room, now a respectable three feet apart. She turned to Caroline first, her eyes friendly and interested.

'Hello. My name is Angie Hall. I'm your predecessor,' she explained smilingly to a confused Caroline, patting the huge bulge of her stomach. 'I'll be training you this week, then I'm going to retire to blissful motherhood. I see you've met Barrett,' she chattered on vivaciously, turning to hang her coat, oblivious to the shocked incredulity of the other two. 'Do you think you'll be happy working for this monster, Mrs Forsythe?'

'Barrett Rossiter?' Caroline swallowed thickly.

'*Mrs* Forsythe?' Barrett gritted out simultaneously, his hand capturing Caroline's and viciously twisting her ring finger up for inspection in a move that could barely pass for a handshake.

'Mrs Forsythe,' he repeated tautly.

Caroline pulled her hand away. 'Mr Rossiter,' she muttered resentfully.

'I thought you two had already met!' Angie Hall was clearly confused.

'I think we just did, Angie,' Barrett responded cryptically, his eyes contemptuous as they studied Caroline's tense features. Abruptly he turned on his heel and flung himself into his office, a snarled, 'One of you get in here for dictation!' thrown over his shoulder before the door of the inner office slammed behind him.

'Well!' Angie blinked. 'I was joking when I called him a monster, but ... What's been going on here? I've never seen Barrett act like that.' She turned expectantly to Caroline.

Caroline forced a stiff, insincere smile. 'Just a bad day,' she offered pathetically.

'He doesn't have them,' Angie denied. 'He's an angel to work for ...'

'Angie!' Barrett barked over the intercom and Caroline jumped.

Angie looked at her oddly. 'Could you go, Mrs Forsythe? I'm not settled yet, and I have to visit the ladies' room.'

Caroline swallowed grimly. She had taken enough 'dictation' from Barrett Rossiter for one day, but what could she do, short of run screaming from the building and from her job?

'Of course,' she answered somewhat blankly. 'Call me Caroline, please.'

Angie smiled. 'And you must call me——'

'Angie!' Barrett's impatient bellow—he had not bothered with the intercom this time—finished the invitation, and Angie giggled.

'You'd better go, Caroline,' she advised, heading towards the door. 'I'll be back in ten minutes.'

Grimly Caroline picked up a shorthand pad and a couple of pencils from the desk and walked to Barrett's door. Counting to ten, she pushed the door open and stepped into the room.

Barrett's sharp eyes halted her in her tracks. 'I asked for Angie,' he reminded her softly, his tone cutting.

'She's in the ladies' room,' Caroline replied with forced politeness, congratulating herself on her steady voice.

'She's always in the ladies' room,' Barrett grumbled.

'She's pregnant,' Caroline offered politely.

'Do you have children, Mrs Forsythe?' he shot at her rudely.

Caroline counted to ten again.

'No,' she answered evenly, having reached the magic number.

'Been married long?' he sneered.

What a question! 'No.'

'Then maybe you've been married such a short period of time that you're not accustomed yet to limiting your—favours,' he suggested cruelly.

Caroline flushed fierily but said nothing, her lips firmly compressed.

Barrett, impatient, ordered her to sit. 'If you're going to take dictation, it might be more comfortable,' he added loftily.

Caroline sat, ignoring the sarcasm, wondering if she should possibly try increasing the count to twenty.

Abruptly Barrett began to dictate at a punishing pace. After an hour Caroline's fingers cramped, and still he did not let up, driving on ruthlessly. Finally, after another forty-five minutes, he stopped, flicking back his cuff to glance at his watch.

'That's it. I've got an appointment in five minutes.'

Caroline jumped up with alacrity, stretching her stiff back gratefully as she moved to the door.

'Mrs Forsythe——' Barrett's soft drawl stopped her as her hand reached for the knob and she turned to face him warily. 'I'd like those letters by one o'clock.'

Caroline nodded. It would be a challenge, but she would do it.

Barrett waited until her hand was on the knob once again before adding softly, 'In French, German and Spanish.'

Her mouth fell open in astonishment, but she snapped it shut determinedly. He was waiting for a protest, she knew, and she was determined not to give him that satisfaction.

'Of course, Mr Rossiter,' she answered smoothly, her slightly surprised tone indicating that she had thought the added instructions superfluous, but was too polite to say so. She would get the letters done if she had to skip lunch to do it! 'If there's nothing else . . .?' she prompted sweetly.

'No, I think that's quite enough, Mrs Forsythe,' Barrett shot back, his tone rich with sadistic satisfaction.

Caroline bit her lip to prevent the sarcastic rejoinder that hovered there from escaping and silently left the room.

The satisfied smirk left Barrett's face as the door closed behind her. A soft stream of expletives rolled steadily off his tongue. Married! And Waxler had known it, damn him. That explained the secretive, gloating expression on his face all week. Barrett had won the battle, but Ronald Waxler had purposely neglected to tell him that there was no war.

Barrett had never touched a married woman, and he was not about to start now. The complications were too great, but the main issue was a moral one. Certain areas in Barrett's reasoning had never escaped the shading of black and white. When it came to marriage, there were no greys. It was an institution he respected, if not yet sampled, and he would not contribute to its deterioration.

Caroline Forsythe would be a valuable employee— she had proved that already with her ability to keep up with his deliberately accelerated dictation. Barrett would somehow forget anything else he might have pictured her being.

CHAPTER THREE

CAROLINE climbed out of the small car with a confusing clash of emotions warring inside her. She could hardly wait to see Stacy again, after a whole week of talking to her only over the phone, knowing that Stacy couldn't speak naturally with Lawrence monitoring her every word. Caroline needed to reassure herself that Stacy was indeed all right. But the knowledge that she would also be seeing Lawrence again, and asking him for custody of her little sister, filled her with a sinking fear. She was terrified of the cruelty and the violence that raged in him, unappeased.

Stacy was streaking out of the front door and down the steps of the shabby little house before the empty echo of Caroline's slamming car door died.

'Carly!' she called, laughing and crying at the same time as she launched herself into Caroline's open, waiting arms.

Although she was on her knees, braced for Stacy's exuberant greeting, Caroline was rocked on her heels by the force of her sister's weight. After regaining her balance, Caroline's arms closed tightly around Stacy's quivering, thin little body.

'Ah, sweetheart,' she whispered, 'it's so good to see you again!'

'I've missed you so, Carly.' The words were mumbled into Caroline's neck.

'I've missed you too, punkin. But I've been getting settled into my new job and fixing up my apartment . . .' She broke off awkwardly, wary of raising Stacy's hopes. It had always been silently understood between them that when Caroline was finally in a position to support them both, Stacy would come to her. But now Lawrence stood between them and every one of their plans.

Stacy pulled away, leaning back to look into Caroline's face.

'Could I——' she swallowed, 'could I come and live with you, Carly? I'll be real good, I promise. I won't make a mess, and I—I'll wash dishes, and I won't play loud——' she pleaded urgently, her little face tight and desperate as she made promises Caroline would never want her to keep.

'Stacy . . .' Caroline soothed quietly, one hand on Stacy's brown head, 'you know you don't have to make any of those promises. I'd probably go crazy if you behaved yourself!' And then, wanting nothing more than to erase the frightened look from her sister's pale face, she murmured sadly, 'Stacy, I want you to live with me more than anything . . .' A wildly hopeful light brightened Stacy's blue eyes at the words, and Caroline raised a cautioning hand. 'But it's up to . . . Lawrence. We have to have his permission first,' she continued steadily, hiding her own apprehension. 'That's one of the reasons I came today, besides wanting to see you. I want to talk to Lawrence about letting you live with me.'

Stacy's little face became set. 'He won't——'

'Maybe,' Caroline broke in. 'We have to ask.'

A little silence hung between them.

'But first,' Caroline spoke bracingly, 'I want to talk to *you*. Come on, let's go to the garden.' She straightened and held out her hand, her longer legs keeping up easily with Stacy's impulsive skips as they skirted the dilapidated house, with its sagging steps and peeling paint, and crossed the back yard to the little garden their mother had once lovingly tended. In the last years of her life, when Marie had scarcely left her room, it had fallen to Caroline and Stacy to tend the wild profusion of flowers and shrubs. Now, in the cold winter months, it lay dull and lifeless, the brilliance of summer deadened by the unrelenting chill of winter. The same feeling of dull emptiness gripped Caroline as she eyed it sadly. It seemed symbolic somehow, like the wedding band she still wore on her finger.

Collapsing on a small decaying wood bench and pulling Stacy down with her, she drew her coat more tightly around her slender form. It was freezing outside. Feburary had slid quietly into March, with no noticeable change. The snow was gone for now, but Caroline could see her breath vapourising cloudily as it left her mouth. She didn't want to go into the house yet, though. She wasn't ready to face Lawrence.

'How's school?' Caroline asked quietly, real interest in her tone. Stacy was quick, intelligent. She loved her classes, and the enjoyment bubbled out naturally with Caroline, as it did with no one else.

In many ways, the last six years with Lawrence had scarred Stacy too. Not physically, but in a crueller, more lasting way. She was a quiet, secretly lonely person, withdrawn and wary with strangers to an almost painful degree. In a manner way beyond her years, she held people at bay with her cautious, suspicious eyes. Everyone but Caroline. Secure in the steadfastness of her sister's love, Stacy bloomed in Caroline's presence, becoming a lively, blessedly normal seven-year-old.

'School's okay,' she answered with childish non-chalance, her mouth curving mischievously. 'I got a star on my math test and Mrs Tetcher hung our paintings on the wall, and——' here she paused, her eyes darting to Caroline, 'Cindy Hill kissed Matt Cox at recess!' This seemed by far to be the most fascinating event for Stacy.

'And what did Matt Cox say about that?' Caroline questioned gravely.

'He hit her,' Stacy supplied matter-of-factly. 'And Cindy cried and hit him back.'

Caroline's lips twitched slightly. How simple it was when you were seven.

'Have you ever kissed somebody, Carly?' Stacy demanded innocently.

A strange flashing picture of the kiss Barrett Rossiter had planted on her unsuspecting mouth that first day,

and of the disturbing sensations he had aroused,
crawled into Caroline's mind. She wanted desperately
to be able to forget it, but it came back to haunt her at
the oddest times—when Barrett was behind his desk,
shooting rapid-fire orders at her, as she dried herself
after a long, luxurious bath, trying to avert her eyes
from her body in the mirror, and now, here with Stacy,
who was studying her avidly for just such a reaction. As
always, the memory induced a fine trembling in her
limbs, and etched a frightened vulnerability in her eyes
that Caroline was completely unaware of. The
vulnerability was there now. Stacy saw and recognised
it instinctively.

'Have you?' she prompted eagerly.

'Yes,' Caroline answered honestly, her mind still
warring with her traitorous body.

'Did you hit him after?' The subject was apparently
too fascinating to drop.

'No. But I wanted to,' Caroline answered feelingly,
remembering the fury and fright at her own response.

'Didn't you like it?' Stacy's thin face fell disap-
pointedly.

'Yes, I liked it . . .'

'Well then——' Stacy began with the determined
logic of a seven-year-old.

'But he shouldn't have kissed me. He had no right,'
Caroline finished firmly.

'What gives someone the right to kiss you?' Stacy
demanded interestedly.

'Oh . . .' Caroline began, feeling she had got in over
her head, but unable to stem the flow of her sister's
innocent questions. 'If you like someone, and want him
to kiss you, or if you're engaged or married——'

'Lawrence was married to Mom . . .' Stacy muttered
bleakly.

Caroline's arm slipped comfortingly around the thin
shoulders. 'Yes, he was.'

'I don't remember him kissing her,' Stacy continued
flatly. 'And she never kissed him.'

How can I explain to her? Caroline wondered bitterly. How can I make her understand love—this love that bound their mother for ever to Robert Forsythe, or the 'love' that twisted Lawrence into brutality? How can I explain something I don't understand myself?

'Sometimes,' she began carefully, 'people can only ever love once——'

'Like Mom loved Dad,' Stacy translated, her little face sombre.

'Like Mom loved Dad.' Caroline agreed.

Stacy was silent for a moment, obviously thinking.

'Does that mean she didn't love us?' she asked finally.

'Oh, honey, no!' Caroline denied instantly, drawing Stacy into her arms and holding her close. 'Mom loved us. It was a different kind of love, that's all.'

'Are there many kinds of love, Carly?' Stacy's voice was muffled now.

'There are probably as many different kinds of love as there are different kinds of people, Stacy,' Caroline answered softly, her mind once more playing over her reaction to Barrett's kiss. Surely that ... Oh my God, she prayed sickly, surely that wasn't love!

Stacy's arms wound tightly around Caroline's neck.'I love you, Carly,' she whispered.

Caroline's eyes closed. 'I love you too, Stacy.' And somehow, she vowed silently, I will find a way to get custody, to get you away from Lawrence. Far away where he can never hurt either of us again.

'Hey, come on,' she cried, pulling back from Stacy's arms, a wobbly smile twisting her lips as she sought to bring them away from the precipice of emotion they were balanced on. 'We're supposed to be happy to be together, and here we sit, crying like a couple of babies! Let's go for for a walk.'

Stacy giggled in an embarrassed way, rubbing at her grimy cheeks. 'I'm sorry, Carly, I didn't mean to cry. But I do love you.'

'And I love you, Stacy. That's not something to cry about. Right?'

'Right,' Stacy agreed happily. 'Let's go to the park.'

So hand in hand they strolled to the nearby park. For an hour they forgot the sadness of the past, the uncertainty of the future, and lost themselves in the simple outdoor pleasures of swinging and climbing monkey bars and running through wide open fields. Caroline became a child again, playing with the same innocent, boisterous unselfconsciousness of her seven-year-old sister. Indulgent, almost envious smiles were directed at her by more restrained adults, as they witnessed her antics.

'Come on, munchkin,' Caroline ordered, catching Stacy's running form and wrestling her to the ground one last time, it's time to go back.'

A little of the happiness died from both glowing faces as the words hung between them. Determinedly picking themselves up and dusting each other off, they headed back to Lawrence's house. Stacy chattered still, but her words rang slightly hollow, and Caroline's answering smiles trembled at the edges. Neither was ready to relinquish the happiness of the other's company, both fearing what waited for them when they faced Lawrence again.

'Well, well,' Lawrence murmured nastily as they entered the house, the storm door noisily latching behind them, 'if it isn't my two little gypsy wanderers, finally come home!'

Stacy's cold hand crept nervously into Caroline's.

Lawrence lay sprawled on the broken down pea-green couch pushed haphazardly against one wall. The room was dingy, despite the late afternoon sunlight fighting to penetrate the grime-streaked windows. The room was almost painfully neat—Stacy straightened up uncomplainingly every day after school, Caroline knew. And probably even more so this Saturday, she speculated wearily, because of her visit. Stacy was possessed of an almost frightening dignity regarding such matters.

'Hello, Lawrence,' Caroline managed calmly for Stacy's sake. 'I'm sorry we left without telling you. We just—forgot.'

Lawrence's light blue eyes sharpened dangerously at the unthinking words, moving from one flushed face to the other, noting the linked hands and Caroline's protective stance beside her little sister.

'Forgot?' he repeated now. 'Forgot me? Surely not, Caroline. I thought I'd managed to leave my—mark in your memory,' he insinuated slyly.

Caroline flinched visibly, the memory of his previous cruelties betraying her. Then seeing the satisfied smirk twisting Lawrence's thick mouth as he witnessed her involuntary reaction, she stiffened.

'Where did you go?' he asked now, the question directed at Stacy.

'We—we went to the park,' she answered hesitantly, her eyes guarded.

'Ah. Did you have fun?' Lawrence persisted, for some unknown reason of his own pretending an indulgent interest.

'Yes,' Stacy answered warily. 'We swung and played tag.'

'Good. You must be tired. Go take a nap, Stacy,' he ordered quietly, his eyes now turned on Caroline.

Caroline squeezed Stacy's hand reassuringly. 'Go ahead, sweetheart,' she directed softly, dropping to her knees on the threadbare carpet to hug Stacy closely. 'I'll see you before I leave.'

Stacy nodded tightly, her eyes full of fearful questions as she thought of the discussion that would soon take place between Caroline and Lawrence—the course of which would determine her future.

'Cross your fingers,' she whispered childishly, for Caroline's ears alone.

Caroline smiled slightly in acknowledgement.

'Go, Stacy,' Lawrence's steely tone broke the contact between the sisters.

Reluctant steps took Stacy to the doorway of her

bedroom. Her hand rested on the doorknob when she turned impulsively. 'I'll see you before you leave, Carly?' she almost begged, her voice desperate.

'You betcha,' Caroline promised. 'Go to bed now.' This as she read the nasty gleam in their stepfather's eyes.

As the door closed softly behind Stacy's little figure, Lawrence turned to Caroline.

'Touching,' he sneered. *'Carly.'*

Caroline rose to her feet, feeling at a distinct disadvantage on her knees.

'Don't ever take her away from this house again,' Lawrence continued, his voice too soft.

'I'm sorry,' Caroline apologised again, nervously brushing the knees of her blue jeans.

'Is my floor too dirty for your pristine body, Caroline?'

Her hands stilled immediately.

'Of—of course not,' she denied, knowing she was not in a position to offend him. 'It's the dirt from the park——'

'Why did you come, Caroline?' Lawrence cut in harshly. 'I thought you were too busy with your new job and your new apartment.'

'I don't have to work on Saturdays, Lawrence, and I—I wanted to see Stacy and ask——'

'You've seen her,' he interrupted rudely. 'Go.'

'And I wanted to ask you something,' she finished with unswerving determination.

'Ask. Then go.'

'You said—you told me that when I got a job and an apartment you would give me custody of Stacy,' she managed tightly.

'And?' Lawrence was not going to make it easy.

'I have a job. I have an apartment . . . I want Stacy.' There, it was out!

A derisive laugh was torn from Lawrence's lips.

'You've had your job less than a week. I think we'll just leave it for a while, little Caroline, until we're sure you're going to stick with this job, hmm?'

'I will stick with it! I like my job——' Caroline protested.

'And does your boss "like" you?' Lawrence asked meaningfully.

'What—what does that mean?' she swallowed thickly.

'Simply that however much you like your job, it's up to your boss to decide whether or not it *remains* your job,' Lawrence answered innocently. 'What else could I have meant?'

'Nothing,' she answered quickly. 'But—I won't be fired, Lawrence I'm sure of it. I'm doing a good job. There's no point in waiting to give me cust——'

'I said leave it!' Lawrence snarled viciously. 'Don't push your luck, little girl.'

'I . . . told Stacy I was going to ask,' she began with difficulty. 'I hoped she could come home with me tonight.'

'No,' he rejected the plea flatly, the sharp negative brooking no argument, but still Caroline persisted.

'Even if she can't come to live with me tonight, couldn't she spend a couple of days with me——?' she pleaded.

Lawrence's expression became uglier. 'No, Caroline. She stays here until I say otherwise.'

Brutal hands closed punishingly around her vulnerable neck, cutting into the words she was about to speak. 'Shut up,' Lawrence ordered harshly. 'If you want to be with Stacy so damn much, move back here.'

'I can't,' Caroline choked hoarsely past his hold on her tender throat as Lawrence watched in sadistic satisfaction. The thought of living in the same house with Lawrence again made her physically sick.

'Don't you want to be near your dear stepfather?' he lamented cruelly, his fingers tightening deliberately around her neck.

'Quit. Come and take care of your little sister and me. Just like your dear mother,' his voice dropped menacingly.

'I'm not my mother,' Caroline spoke shakily.

'No, you're not, are you, little Caroline?' His jagged nails dug into her neck, drawing faint pinpricks of blood. 'She used to cower from me, but you don't cower from anybody, do you, brave little Caroline? You stand there and ask for more. I'll give you more. I'll punish you to hell and back,' he promised thickly.

'I didn't do anything!' she protested, her eyes clouded with fear and confusion, helpless in the hold of his violence. 'Let me go, Lawrence. Let me go!'

He studied her intently, assessing the fear in her pale face. Satisfied, he flung her away. Caroline's body met the hardness of the door violently, her face cracking against its unforgiving surface as the knob rammed painfully into her ribs.

'Go!' Lawrence spat. 'Get out of my sight, you sanctimonious little bitch!'

Caroline's eyes remained shut in agony, the left side of her bruised and throbbing, her tender ribs making each breath drawn torture.

'I have to see Stacy,' she protested thickly, her mind working slowly, dazedly. 'I promised her . . .'

She stumbled towards the bedroom door, but was jerked to a painful stop as one beefy hand dug painfully into her upper arm, bruising its softness.

'Don't scare the poor child,' Lawrence warned quietly, his hand tightening in emphasis. 'You won't, will you, Caroline?' Again the hold tightened.

'No,' she whispered tightly, 'I won't . . .'

'Good,' he smiled urbanely, releasing her arm to reach up and pat her affectionately on her bruised cheek. 'Go and tell your sister goodnight.'

Caroline pushed Stacy's door open then closed it softly behind her. Crossing to the bed, she sat down on the side, noting Stacy's fluttering lids as she pretended to sleep. How much had she heard? Caroline wondered despairingly.

'Stacy,' she whispered hoarsely.

Stacy's eyes flew open. 'Carly! I thought it might

be—him. What did he say? Can I come home with you?' The words spilled out urgently.

Caroline swallowed painfully. 'He—we think it might be better if you stayed—here for a little longer,' she spoke gently, her anguished eyes taking in Stacy's fallen expression.

'He said no.' Stacy was not deceived.

'Stacy . . .'

A sob escaped Caroline involuntarily and Stacy's young brown eyes grew grim.

'Did he hurt you, Carly?' she demanded in a strangely adult tone, her fingers caressing Caroline's cheek soothingly.

Caroline hauled the trembling little body close to her own.

'He can't hurt me, Stacy,' she murmured reassuringly. 'Just like he can never really hurt you.'

They sat like that for a long time, two frightened children huddled close together, seeking shelter from a storm.

'I have to go,' Caroline said at last, pulling away reluctantly and wiping the tears from her cheeks before Stacy saw them. Stacy would be safe, Caroline knew. If there was any chance of Lawrence touching her little sister, Caroline would get her away any way she could.

'I promise I'll be back soon. And—and I'll ask him again, Stacy.'

Stacy nodded dejectedly, releasing her hold. As Caroline reached the door, her shaking voice sliced the silence of the room. 'I'm sorry if he hurt you because of me, Carly.'

Caroline's voice broke as she answered. 'It's not your fault, honey. Never, never think that.'

Stacy did not answer.

'Goodnight, Stacy.' Caroline's voice shattered the darkness.

'Goodnight, Carly.'

Lawrence wasn't in the living room when Caroline

left Stacy's bedroom. Caroline didn't look for him. Silently, she left the house, and climbed back into her car.

On Monday morning Caroline looked into her mirror and groaned. The bruises from Lawrence's brutal hands were visibly brilliant. Her left jaw was darkly shaded from the slamming contact with the door, her ribs were coloured a massive blue-black-yellow combination where the doorknob had gouged her. Smudged fingerprints marred the creamy surface of her neck, and a dark ring circled her upper right arm.

How could she go to work looking like this? she wondered helplessly. What would people think? What would Barrett say?

Caroline's sagging shoulders squared. She had to go in. Barrett was in the middle of acquisition talks with a major French firm, and he needed her assistance.

With a heavy hand she applied her make-up, hiding the bruises on her face as best she could. She would dress to cover the rest. She pulled a high-necked, long-sleeved dress from her closet. Thank goodness it was winter, she thought humourlessly. She would suffocate if she had to wear this smothering tent in the heat of a Denver summer.

If her gait was slightly stiff because of the pain of her ribs, and her expression wooden with caution, nobody seemed to notice and Caroline made it through the morning with reasonable success.

As the afternoon wore on, however, her body began to protest. Her eyes strayed to the clock often. Barrett was in an unusually foul mood—even for him—and she couldn't wait to get home and into a steaming hot tub.

Inevitably, Barrett's keen eyes noticed her distraction.

Collecting a stack of letters she had just finished typing, Caroline knocked on his office door.

'Come,' the gruff order penetrated the door.

Charming, Caroline thought dryly. What manners! she marvelled silently. And what charm school did you graduate from?

Keeping her face expressionless, she laid the papers on his desk. 'These letters need your signature,' she murmured, even as she was turning back towards the connecting door.

'Stay,' he ordered harshly.

Caroline turned slowly, eyeing his downbent head dispassionately. She wondered when he would manage a complete sentence, or at least a word of two syllables.

The silence stretched between them as Barrett bent over the letters, scanning their contents. Caroline stole an impatient glance at her watch. Thirty-five minutes until she could escape.

'Are you in a hurry, Mrs Forsythe?' Barrett enquired silkily, his cold grey eyes meeting hers head on.

Caroline did not answer, and Barrett's eyebrows rose in imperious demand.

'No,' she said repressively.

He rose to his feet then, moving from behind the desk to stand beside her stiffening body. His hand lifted to her face, one long finger flicking her cheek lightly.

Caroline jumped nervously, and Barrett's eyes narrowed.

'You have a smudge on your cheek,' he explained tauntingly.

The bruises! she panicked. The make-up would have begun to fade by now, and she had not thought to touch it up.

'Probably carbon,' she invented hurriedly. 'I'll—I'll go wash it off.' She backed away warily.

'No need.' Barrett's commanding tone stopped her in her tracks. She watched, wide-eyed, as he pulled a sparkling white handkerchief from his jacket pocket and stepped towards her. 'I'll wipe it off.'

'No!' she cried. 'Don't!'

He studied her incredulously, amazed by her reaction. 'I won't hurt you,' he promised indulgently, secretly relishing having finally broken through the ice she had surrounded herself with. 'Stand still.'

Caroline was rooted to the spot, fear paralysing her

body. She watched as Barrett lifted the handkerchief to her cheek, then closed her eyes tightly as he gently rubbed at the bruise.

The motion stopped abruptly. Caroline reluctantly opened her eyes. Barrett's grey eyes were narrowed dangerously as he studied the bruise he had exposed. His angry eyes lifted to meet hers, a silent question in their depths.

Caroline turned blindly towards the door, unable to bear his questions.

'Not so fast——' Barrett bit out, catching one arm tightly and yanking her back to face him, his fingers closing punishingly on the bruises Lawrence had inflicted.

A strangled gasp tore from Caroline's throat, and Barrett's jaw tautened grimly. He released his hold immediately.

Pushing her sleeves up mercilessly, he studied the ugly marks she had made no effort to hide with make-up. His mouth held tight in control, his flaming eyes rose to her face.

'Are there more?' he asked tightly.

Caroline did not answer.

'Where?' he persisted, his voice hard and cold.

'My—my neck,' she whispered in defeat, past caring. 'My ribs.'

'Who did this to you?' he demanded viciously, his razor eyes cutting through her apathy.

'I—I fell,' she invented wildly, wary of the vengeful glare in those darkened eyes and the dangerous tautness of his jaw.

'Try again,' he ordered disbelievingly.

'I fell,' she insisted, her eyes glittering brightly with fear.

Barrett studied her for a long, smothering moment. Raising his hand to her face, he brushed her bruised cheek with gentle fingers.

'I can help you,' he whispered, his eyes meeting hers fiercely. 'Tell me who——'

'I fell! Please—please, Barrett, leave me alone!'

'God, no, I'm not going to leave you alone!' he rasped in a strangled voice. 'I'm going to find out who did this to you and I'm going to——' he broke off abruptly as a thought hit him. 'Or do I have to ask who did this, Caroline?' he demanded grimly. 'It was your husband, wasn't it? God, talk about being slow on the uptake——'

'Barrett,' Caroline begged tiredly, unconsciously using his first name again, 'please leave me alone. Forget about this.'

'Forget about it?' he snarled. 'And you—are you going to "forget about" it?'

'I have to,' she replied dully, almost too weary to speak. She suspected she would collapse to the floor in a heap were it not for Barrett's supporting hands. 'I have no choice.'

'Of course you have a choice!' he exploded wrathfully. 'Get out! Leave him! No man, no marriage is worth this.'

Caroline knew he was speaking about her mythical husband, but her mind was occupied with Lawrence. 'I have to stay, don't you see that?' she told him shrilly, betrayed by the pain of her bruises and her tortured thoughts. 'I can't just walk away, not while I——' abruptly she broke off, catching herself before she blurted out the whole sorry story. She did not want Barrett to think was was begging for his sympathy.

'Leave me alone, Barrett,' she pleaded again. 'Please leave me alone.'

The frustrated violence in his eyes did not soften at her broken plea.

'Go!' he ordered roughly, 'if you like being abused so much, go! I wouldn't want you to miss a second of it,' he added nastily.

Caroline hesitated. 'It's not five o'clock yet.'

'Get the hell out of here, Caroline, before I add some bruises of my own.'

The very softness of his words terrified her. She fled.

CHAPTER FOUR

DAYS dragged past, soldier-slow, blurring into one fast-moving collage of high-powered meetings, frantic deadlines, and hostile coldness. A wall of ice seemed to have sprung up between Barrett and Caroline. Not one word was mentioned about the bruises he had uncovered, but his eyes, when he looked at her, were cutting, silver blades of dislike and contempt. His mouth was drawn in a perpetual grim line, his face hard and edged with violence. Each sentence was deliberately calculated to tear with steely, rending claws. Caroline realised, bewilderedly, that the cold rage was aimed solely at her, but the waves of hostility spilled over to every one unfortunate enough to cross Barrett's path. Even Barrett's top executives, men and women who had previously breezed into his office to share a joke or seek advice on matters both personal and professional, became noticeably scarce. When absolutely necessary, they crept in stealthily, usually at a time when Barrett was known to be out of the building, and dropped the required information on Caroline's desk. They lingered only long enough to cast a pitying glance at her, and a fearful one at the closed door of Barrett's office before scuttling thankfully away again.

Caroline was at a loss. She did not know what she had done to provoke such intense dislike. Surely the discovery of those fast-fading bruises had not brought out this dark violence? Why should Barrett Rossiter care if she set herself up as someone's whipping boy anyway? And why did she care what he thought anyway? she asked herself resentfully. The questions remained unanswered, though, as the rage remained unappeased, and Caroline simply did not know how to deal with Barrett's chill fury. In the beginning she had tried to excuse his behaviour, telling herself that he was just having a bad day, that he was preoccupied with the takeover they were currently embroiled in, that he wasn't feeling well ... Caroline made excuses until she ran out of excuses. And still she somehow remained outwardly untouched by his biting sarcasm.

Then, one day, her control snapped.

An error had been made in the cost estimates sent up from accounting in relation to the proposed takeover. By the time the mistake had been discovered, reports had been typed, bids tendered, supplies ordered. When the error had finally been brought to his attention by the unfortunate accountant responsible, Barrett had erupted. He tore into the man, his words deadly venom. And after the poor man had slinked miserably from the office, Barrett turned on Caroline. Why hadn't *she* discovered the mistake? What the hell did he pay her for anyway? And on and on and on.

'If I have to beat it into you, by God I will!' Barrett ground out, his eyes dark with dislike as he studied the stiff back Caroline presented to him.

It was the last words that cracked her iron reserve. Beat it into her! Never, never would another man lay a hand on her in violence. She rounded on him wildly, her green eyes spitting fire.

'No, Mr Rossiter, you will not beat it into me!' she hissed fiercely. 'But I'd like to beat you! Yes, I would! My God, I've never met such an arrogant—self-satisfied—disgusting bastard in my life! Do you think your employees, *anyone* likes you for the way you treat them? You ought to be shot for the condescending, contemptuous way you talk to us. Yes, we make mistakes! We're human! Can you say the same thing?'

By the time Caroline's tirade had wound down, her whole body was trembling with rage—her breasts heaved, her face was flushed, her hands clenched. A wild surge of adrenalin sang through her body. She was not sorry for her words, and she did not back away from the rage flaring to life in his silver eyes.

Barrett remained curiously still during the entire diatribe, his eyes moving over Caroline intently, taking in every scrap of evidence of her arousal. When she had finished her sweeping condemnation of him and his methods, when no more words spewed forth, his eyes finally lifted to her face, a strange, icy triumph in their depths. With one sentence he annihilated her, his face a savage mask.

Caroline never risked such a confrontation again. Barrett's temper improved somewhat after that incident, but it still buzzed out of control at times, and Caroline was always the target of his cutting rage. She learned to remain impassive, contenting herself with a few well-chosen, heartfelt mutterings in some obscure foreign language he was sure not to understand.

But more than the weight of Barrett's biting anger was wearing her down. She had been working for him three weeks, and each Saturday since her job began she had gone to visit Stacy, each time asking Lawrence for custody, only to be informed that he still wanted to wait until he was sure her job was 'secure'.

Stacy had even ceased to ask about it any more, her small face closed. She had given up hope, Caroline knew, and the sight of her grimly resigned eyes tore at Caroline mercilessly.

She didn't know how much longer either of them could take the strain. Stacy was suffering, but Caroline did not know how to ease the pain. Lawrence had not said that Stacy could never live with Caroline, only that she couldn't leave him now. And while there was even the slightest chance that Lawrence would sign over custody legally, Caroline hesitated to take any precipitate action that might spoil her chances. Sometimes she felt that Lawrence was merely playing with her for his own amusement, dangling Stacy before her like a red cape before a bull, but Caroline could not be sure.

So for three long weeks Caroline and Stacy were locked in that agonising limbo of doubt and denied hope. Nothing changed. Lawrence drank heavily, but he never laid a finger on Stacy, and Caroline was not available. He took out his rage on walls and strangers, before stumbling home and passing out.

But Caroline felt instinctively that the period of stagnation was coming to an end, that something would change, and soon. She didn't know if any of them would be able to live with the change.

It happened three days later. In the space of twenty-four hours, Caroline's world was rocked on its axis, never to right itself again.

She was late. Her alarm clock, for some perverse reason of its own, failed to sound. Jack-knifing out of bed, she showered in less than three minutes. Paying scant attention to her hair and make-up, she threw her clothes on haphazardly, barely taking time to do buttons and ties. She skipped breakfast entirely, intent on reaching her bus stop before the bus.

She ran the entire two blocks to her stop, earning herself only a painful stitch in her side and a tantalising glimpse of the back of the bus as it turned the corner three blocks ahead.

'Damn, damn, damn!' she cursed with a distinct lack of imagination or flair. 'I'll have to take the car.' She turned on her heel, stalking back towards her apartment.

She sat in her little Toyota for five minutes trying to start it, but the engine refused to turn over. Her fists clenched whitely in frustration. It had to start! It didn't. Another ten minutes were wasted in fruitless effort, the only result being the flooding of the engine.

She swung out of the car, slamming the door with healthy violence behind her. As she glided past the misbehaving vehicle, she couldn't resist one final kick at the tyre. Unfortunately, on the downward swing, her leg scraped along the rough edge of the back bumper. She groaned at the soft shredding sound of her pantyhose as they caught, and a wide ladder merrily zipped its way along her leg.

Muttering uncharitable remarks about hose in

general, and this pair in particular, Caroline stripped
off, stuffing them in her bag as she left the garage
and headed once again for the bus stop. She would take
the next bus, and change her tights at the office, where
she kept an extra pair in her desk drawer. With luck
Barrett would be too busy yelling at her for her
tardiness to notice her bare legs.

Barrett. Another groan was forced from her lips, this
one louder than the last. He would kill her. He would
chew her up and spit her out in tiny pieces.

By the time the bus arrived, Caroline was forty-five
minutes late. She sank thankfully into a seat, grateful
for the warmth of the bus after fifteen minutes of
pacing in the biting winter wind of early morning
Denver without tights.

As the bus slowly plodded towards town, Caroline
amused herself by devising suitably gruesome fates for
her doomed alarm clock. Throwing it away wasn't
enough, she decided with a bloodthirsty vengeance.
She would crack it open with a hammer—a sledge-
hammer—and pour a gallon of acid over its inner
workings. The image satisfied her immensely. She
didn't bother to wonder where she was going to
acquire a gallon of acid. Caroline's imagination
blazed as her temper blazed, but neither held any real
malice.

By the time she reached the office building, she was
an hour late. As she crossed the lobby and headed to
the elevator that would take her to the office suite she
shared with Barrett. Besides the fact that Caroline
Forsythe was never late, she was never less than
perfectly groomed either. Now, with her glorious hair
wind-tousled, and the colour the winter chill had
presumably whipped in her cheeks, she looked quite . . .
abandoned. Jenny Wilkins allowed herself one moment
of jealousy before greeting Caroline.

'Good morning, Caroline. Horrible weather,' she
murmured, trying to dredge some semblance of
sincerity into her words.

'Good morning, Jenny. Yes, it is bad,' Caroline agreed automatically as she stepped into the elevator.

The receptionist watched enviously as the doors closed and the elevator made its way to the penthouse suite. All that, she thought waspishly, and Barrett Rossiter, too. Oh, she knew that Caroline Forsythe was married, but rumours swept wildly through the building about her and the boss. Jenny herself had seen them together, and with an insight very rare for her, had sensed the almost electric awareness that flashed between them.

Caroline, completely unaware of Jenny's thoughts, was standing in front of the office door with her hand on the knob. Buck up, she told herself encouragingly, he can only fire you. Squaring her shoulders determinedly, she opened the door to the outer office and stepped in.

Steely grey eyes swivelled to halt her in her place, freezing her with one icy glance before she had even closed the door behind her. The man leaning calmly against her desk, obviously waiting for her arrival, flicked one dark brow in silent demand, infuriating her.

She could not move as his eyes swept measuringly over her, feeling trapped, pinned, she thought resentfully, like a butterfly on the end of a collector's needle. Seething, she slammed the door sharply behind her and moved stiffly to the coat rack, acutely conscious of his hard eyes following her, assessing her.

'You're late,' his harsh voice informed her, as though doubting she was aware of the fact, and she turned to him, an explanation on her lips. 'Sixty-eight minutes late,' the cold voice went on, narrowed eyes not even glancing at the thin gold watch on his wrist to verify the time. 'I hope it was good, at least.'

Caroline quivered. 'I don't know what you're talking about,' she answered arctically. 'My alarm didn't go off. I'm sorry.' She threw the words at him, a challenge.

Barrett's eyes glinted. 'Come, come, *Mrs* Forsythe, I'm a grown man. I understand the urges that overtake

two people. . . . even at the most inconvenient of times.'
Caroline's cheeks became a fiery red as his meaning at
last became clear. Metal grey eyes noted the blush and
turned mocking. 'You have nothing to be ashamed of,
Caroline. After all, it's quite legal,' he ground the words
out viciously, his eyes dangerous.

'I've explained why I'm late,' Caroline answered,
ignoring the taunt.

Barrett's face became menacing as he was deliberately
ignored. 'Your husband seems to be lacking in
technique,' he began in retaliation. 'Apart from the fact
that you look as though you've just been dragged
backwards through a bush, he seems to have left no
lasting impression. If it weren't for the fact that your
hair is a mess, and your blouse is unbuttoned——'
Caroline's shocked gasp cut into his words, her hands
flying to the front of her silky shirt, '—you'd look as
cool and remote as you always do. Maybe he needs
some lessons,' Barrett finished deliberately, his eyes on
the swell of her breasts visible through the gaping
material.

'Not from you!' Caroline snapped tightly, goaded
into response.

'Why not from me?' he shot back. 'I got a response
like a tidal wave that first day.'

'I do not wish to talk about that day,' Caroline
informed him frigidly, her face flaming.

'No, let's not talk about it. You'd probably try to
deny that, too,' Barrett agreed derisively. 'Let's talk
about your morning's entertainment with your husband.
Tell me, Caroline,' he probed cruelly, 'is he as brutal in
bed as he is out of it?'

'I have no intention of taking part in this
conversation,' she told him muffledly.

'All right, *Mrs* Forsythe,' he stressed savagely. 'Hide
from yourself if you want, but you can't hide from me.'

Caroline met his scornful eyes, wary and confused. 'I
don't know what you're talking about——'

'Don't you?' he cut in relentlessly. Then, his eyes

studying her face, he conceded tautly. 'No, you probably don't at that.' He straightened from the desk and slammed into his office, throwing the order, 'Get to work,' over his shoulder.

By the time the hands of the clock crept to five o'clock, Caroline's nerves were ragged. Her cheeks ached with the effort of maintaining a stiffly bland expression in the face of Barrett's sarcastic, cutting temper. He bit out orders, using words with the deadly precision of a surgeon's scalpel. Caroline almost expected to find blood seeping from her verbally lashed body after each of their confrontations.

Gathering up the last stack of letters for signing, she knocked on the closed door separating the two offices.

'Come.'

She opened the door and crossed to his desk, eyes wary. Barrett's dark head was bent over the file in his hands, his eyes skimming across it rapidly. He said nothing as she placed the letters on his desk. Caroline waited awkwardly for his attention, the silence stretching her nerves tautly.

'Yes, Caroline?' he prompted softly, his eyes not moving from the paper in his hands.

'It's five o'clock. I'm going now.' The words were terse, barely within the limits of professional politeness.

Barrett's head raised sharply. 'By all means,' he agreed viciously, his dark face edged with violence. 'Maybe you can pick up where you left off this morning.'

Caroline drew a deep, angry breath. 'Mr Rossiter——' the name was forced past clenched teeth, 'I do not have to take this abuse from you.' Turning sharply, she stormed from Barrett's office.

'No, you don't have to take abuse from me, do you, Caroline?' he taunted cruelly, hot on her heels. 'You can go home and get it from your husband!'

Caroline whitened. My God, she thought half-hysterically, there's nothing like going straight for the jugular!

Grabbing her bag from a desk drawer, she marched to the door that led into the hallway, only to be brought up short as she registered Barrett's reclining length against her escape hatch.

'Get out of my way,' she ordered tightly, her composure completely shattered and with it the ability to remain aloof and cold.

'So eager to collect more bruises, Caroline?' he sneered. 'My God, do you *like* being abused?'

'You know nothing about it,' she told him in a strangled tone, her throat clenching spasmodically.

'Then tell me!' he invited bitterly. 'Tell me why you stay with him. Tell me you love him, even after he does this——' one long finger swept contemptuously to the fast-fading bruise on her temple. 'Tell me you want to go home to him.'

'I don't!' she shouted harshly, goaded beyond all endurance. 'I don't want to go back to him. I don't love him!'

Barrett's hands closed punishingly on her shoulders. 'Then why?' he demanded, shaking her for emphasis. 'Why do you stay?'

'I have to,' she whispered shakily, thinking of Stacy. 'I have to stay.'

'I'll help you, Caroline,' Barrett promised roughly, his eyes dark and intent on her tormented features. 'Whatever it takes, I'll help you. I'll find you someplace to live——'

'No!' Caroline denied, denied the temptation to lose herself in his comforting words, denied his right to offer such comfort, denied herself something she could not— would not—name. 'I don't need anything from you——'

'Oh, you need something all right,' he told her violently, his fingers twisting around the loose, silky tendrils of her hair and jerking her head up to study her frightened face. 'You need some sense pounded into that empty, scared head of yours.' His grey eyes flamed dangerously as they locked on her trembling lips. 'And I'm just the man to do it . . .'

'No!' Caroline yelled, reading the frustrated intent in his face. 'Don't——!'

Her words were smothered under the hot possession of his marauding lips as they claimed hers. He ravaged her savagely, his mouth cruel as he punished her for some unspoken wrong.

Caroline fought him desperately, trying to twist her lips from beneath his, but Barrett would not allow the freedom. With his hands still wound in her hair, he held her head still, biting her bottom lip sharply in explicit warning as she continued to struggle. The taste of her own blood mingled tightly with the scorching pain Barrett was inflicting, both physical and emotional. Tears slipped heedlessly from her eyes, sliding slowly down her cheeks and meeting his skin.

At the feel of the damp tears, Barrett ripped his mouth from hers, raising his head a scant inch to speak.

'Damn you!' he gritted roughly. 'I don't want to hurt you!'

Her eyes met his sightlessly, blinded by pain and fear.

With a tortured groan, Barrett's mouth claimed hers again, but now his lips healed instead of hurt, soothed rather than punished, gave pleasure to erase the pain.

Caroline's body was curiously still as she absorbed the new sensations he was arousing with the soft stroking of his lips and hands. She felt the violence draining out of him, a new gentleness taking its place. His lips played pleadingly with hers, not forcing now, but begging for response as his hands gently soothed the frightened stiffness from her limbs.

Caroline could not control the rushing wave of response he ignited, could not deny herself the knowledge and rapture his touch promised. Her lips began to move tentatively beneath his, timidly responding to his touch. Suddenly she ached for the tenderness he offered.

With a smothered sigh of satisfaction, Barrett deepened the kiss, his hand rising to cup the weight of one swelling breast. Caroline drew a shallow, trembling little breath as she felt her body stirring into full arousal, but she could not force her body away from the hot promise of his touch.

Barrett felt the last resistance crumble. Shifting restlessly, he reversed their positions, backing her against the unyielding surface of the door and pressing his hard body against her fully, moulding his blatant demand to the softness of her arching body.

His hand feathered down her straining length, teasing, soothing, arousing needs that Caroline, in her untried innocence, had never suspected existed.

Her own hands lifted yearningly, softly meeting the hard damp skin of his chest beneath his shirt. Her fingers undid the buttons blindly, intent on the feel of his warmth and hardness. A long quivering sigh racked her body as her palms flattened against the stiff peaks of his masculine nipples. She was no longer afraid of Barrett, but of herself, of the raging need he had aroused in her. Tearing herself from his arms, she twisted away, her eyes glittering wildly.

'Caro?' Barrett's voice was thick and urgent as he spoke her name, his eyes hot and stormy black. He took three steps towards her before he was stopped by the burning glare she turned on him.

'No! Don't touch me!' she ordered desperately. 'I hate it. I hate what you're doing to me!'

Barrett flinched from the raw pain in her eyes and voice. His hungry, aroused body did not allow him to follow when Caroline ripped the office door open and flung out of the room, racing for freedom.

As she disappeared around the corner of the elevator bank, his hand slammed violently against the wall, so swamped in the memory of the scene he had just precipitated that he did not notice the jarring pain of his action.

'Damn!' he ground out bitterly.

What in hell had possessed him to go after her like that to hurt her so badly? He ached to prove to her that a man could be gentle, and instead he had savaged her.

I had no right to try to make love to her, Barrett acknowledged grimly, no right to tear her emotions apart. I had no right.

CHAPTER FIVE

CAROLINE dragged herself up the steep flight of bleak stairs that led to her apartment. Her breath came in great, heaving drags, a steel band seeming to close tighter and tighter around her chest. She had no recollection of the trip home from the office. Her mind was focused with such painful clarity on the events of that afternoon—the contemptuous glare of Barrett's eyes, the arousing, frightening passion of his kiss—that she had been blind to everything else.

Her fingers groped numbly for the key to her door, losing their grasp on the chain and dropping it to the floor. Caroline bent wearily, scraping the key up with a trembling hand. As she began to rise, she noticed the thin crack between the jam and the slightly opened door that revealed a slicing view of her living room. The door was open. And probably had been all day! She must not have pulled it shut properly in her rush that morning. How she had hurried to get to work this morning!

Her mouth twisted derisively. She should have stayed home. She would tomorrow. Her expression became rebellious. Nothing—nothing—could force her to face Barrett tomorrow; she could not meet those mocking, knowing eyes, or the sardonic curl of his mouth. What he must think of her—a 'married' woman who responded so completely to another man's advances?

'Coward,' she berated herself, pushing open the door and stepping inside. She flung her handbag on a nearby chair with vicious precision.

As she moved forward, her attention was caught by some flutter of movement across the room. She turned, drawing a deep, uneasy breath, then released it in a defeated sigh as she realised that she had been frightened by her own reflection. Is this what it's come to? she wondered wearily. Will I spend the rest of my life looking over my shoulder for Barrett Rossiter, waiting for the final confrontation?

Moving across the room, she studied her image with fever bright eyes, restlessly taking note of the hectic flush that had mounted in her cheeks, and the bruised tenderness of her mouth.

Game, set and match to you, Mr Rossiter, she conceded woodenly. Enjoy your victory while it lasts.

She raised her hands, running them through her flame-coloured hair, trying to smooth it back into its usual prim style, as if by doing this she could erase the reality of what had happened, the evidence of which lay in the hotly disturbed eyes staring back at her. With a start, she realised that her blouse was partially unbuttoned, revealing the creamy swell of her still taut breasts. She burned with mortification. Had Barrett seen her like this ... burning eyes, aroused body, hungry mouth? She moaned beneath her breath, answering her own question. Of course he'd seen her like this. He had aroused this! I wonder, a new, sneaking voice questioned insidiously, if he'd like what he saw ...

She turned quickly from the mirror, feeling betrayed by her own image. Hurried fingers fumbled with the buttons on her blouse. All she wanted to do now was to hide—from Barrett Rossiter and from herself.

She had taken one step towards her bedroom when a low rustling noise stopped her in her tracks. It came from the tiny kitchen. Her whole body was paralysed as the sound of running water penetrated the door separating the two rooms. A slight hissing sound, then the opening and closing of cupboard doors reached her.

She was frozen to the spot, her heart pounding wildly. For one second she considered the idea of slipping noiselessly from the apartment and going for help. She squared her shoulders determinedly. She had run away from too many things today; she would not run any more. Some part of her that was too tired, too miserable to be scared silently reached for the heavy metal poker resting near the fireplace and inched to the kitchen door, her steps deadened by the worn carpet.

Drawing one deep, calming breath, Caroline raised the poker high above her head and kicked the swinging door open with her foot, ready to challenge the source of the noise.

Leaning nonchalantly against the kitchen counter, facing the door, stood her stepfather, legs crossed casually in front of him.

'Why, Caroline dear, whatever are you doing?' he slurred drunkenly, eyeing the poker in her hand with amusement. 'Is this any way to greet your beloved stepfather?' he smirked.

A shudder passed through Caroline's body as she slowly lowered the weapon and sagged against the door, meeting Lawrence's bloodshot eyes.

'Lawrence,' she breathed incredulously, 'what are you doing here?'

'Making coffee, of course,' he responded mockingly, as though it were something he did every day of his life. 'I know what a little prude you become when I have a couple of drinks.'

'A couple, Lawrence?' she questioned cynically. 'How many is a couple? Five? Seven?' she persisted when he did not answer. 'Do you even remember how many?'

'Just enough to forget, little girl,' he shot back wildly. 'Just enough to forget.'

Caroline closed her eyes briefly, trying to block out his face; the alcohol-slackened mouth, the reddened eyes brimming with a glazed self-pity.

'Tired, little girl?' a sneering voice broke into her thoughts.

Her eyes snapped open. Tired? she pondered cynically. It wasn't the right word. First that scene with Barrett and now . . . this!

'Where do you keep the damn cups, Caroline?' Lawrence cursed indistinctly, his unsteady hands rummaging once again through the cabinets, knocking over glasses.

Caroline crossed the room silently, allowing the kitchen door to swing closed behind her. She reached around her stepfather's bulky form and lifted out an overturned mug directly in front of him.

'Here,' she shoved the mug at him, then sighed with resignation as he stood regarding it with dull incomprehension. She moved to the stove, pouring the now steaming coffee carefully into the cup and offering it once more to her stepfather.

'You wanted coffee,' she enunciated clearly, waiting with a kind of practised patience for him to take the cup.

Lawrence grabbed at it roughly, slopping the scalding liquid on to her hand. She drew back quickly, sucking in a sharp breath. A red stain was already spreading on her hand, and Lawrence's mouth twisted in sadistic pleasure. Caroline flinched but refused to give him the satisfaction of seeing the tears that threatened. She turned stiffly to the sink, running cold water over the reddened area.

A forceful hand slammed the cup of coffee down beside her, almost emptying its contents on the counter.

'I don't want your damn coffee,' Lawrence roared.

She turned to him bravely. 'What *do* you want, Lawrence? And how did you get into my apartment?'

His mouth twisted uglily. 'The door was open, little Caroline. I thought you meant for me to come in,' he replied in slurred reproach, answering her last question.

So she *had* left the door open that morning. Would she never learn? From now on she would make sure the door was kept locked at all times. She never wanted to come home to this again.

She was tired of the verbal fencing. She wanted nothing more than to throw herself on her bed and escape into whatever peace sleep would bring to her. But first there was Lawrence to face. And from the nasty gleam in his eyes she could tell he was spoiling for a fight.

Squaring her shoulders resolutely, she demanded, 'What do you want, Lawrence?'

'Why, Caroline, just to see your smiling face. Though I must say,' he inserted maliciously, 'you do look a little—harried, and that will never do,' he clicked his tongue admonishingly, the twisted smile on his mouth fading and his eyes going deadly still. 'Especially since Stacy has the impression that she's going to be moving in with you soon.'

Caro inhaled deeply. Lawrence was indeed looking for a fight!

'You said—Lawrence, you said that when I found a good job, when I started to earn good money, Stacy could come and live with me. I want her with me, and she wants to be with me.' Caroline's voice took on a vaguely pleading note. 'She's not happy with you, Lawrence. You promised——'

'Ah, but I've changed my mind, you see. Stacy is such a comfort to me . . .' he tormented her slowly, enjoying the pain he was inflicting with such practised sadistic pleasure. 'I don't see how I could possibly let her go.'

'I'll fight you,' she whispered fiercely, determined never to give in where Stacy's happiness was concerned. 'I'll fight you in every way I can, in every court in this land,' she promised hotly.

'And what will you tell them?' Lawrence cut in crudely. 'You're twenty-three years old, you live alone, work all day, and God knows what you do with your nights——'

'You bas——' Caroline bit off harshly, infuriated by the unwarranted attack.

Lawrence continued without pause. 'How could you possibly have the time for the responsible care of a seven-year-old? Whereas I——' he smiled sickly, '—I spend my entire day——'

'Drinking!' she finished for him roughly.

'—at home,' he completed, ignoring her jibe. 'No, Caroline, you'll never get that child, not unless I agree to it. And I don't seem to be in the mood to agree to it,' he ended mockingly.

'I am her sister, Lawrence——'

'And I'm her stepfather. Besides,' he derided cruelly, 'if I let her live with you, poor Stacy will grow up to be as frumpy and repressed as you are.'

Caroline took that without flinching. She'd heard it all before. He'd hammered it into her for years, convincing her—on some level at least—that it was true. When she looked into a mirror, subconsciously her stepfather's malicious assessment clawed at her, blinding her to the beauty and grace she possessed. Instead, she saw the frump he had conditioned her to expect. In a sense, Caroline had been deprived of herself, denied the confidence and assurance everyone needs to be able to truly believe in oneself.

'I'm afraid I can't let that happen to Stacy,' Lawrence continued, shaking his head regretfully. 'It's my duty as her stepfather to——'

'Your duty!' Caroline bit out rawly. 'You forgot your duty when Mother died!'

Lawrence's bloodshot eyes narrowed with menace. 'Watch it, little Caroline. I might "forget" to let you see Stacy ever again.'

'You wouldn't!' she breathed thickly. 'You can't!'

'Can't I?' he mocked relentlessly. 'Unless you can teach her how to leave a trail of breadcrumbs . . .'

'My God! Even you,' her lip curled with contempt, 'even you couldn't be that cruel!'

'No?' he drawled softly.

'Lawrence, you loved my mother. I know you did.' Lawrence watched, unmoved, as she began to plead with him. 'It's not a kind of love that I——' here she faltered, searching desperately for words. 'It's not a kind of love that I can understand—you always seemed to be looking for ways to hurt her—but I know that you loved her in your way. For Mother's sake,' she implored dispairingly, 'for the sake of your love for her——' she was interrupted by his bitter shout of laughter. Looking into his bleary eyes, gleaming with cruel contempt, Caroline knew that she had not reached him, had not touched him. She despised herself for begging with him, for she would never beg for herself. Stacy, she told herself firmly. This is for Stacy.

She tried another tack. 'Surely when you look at Stacy, you see Mother. They're so much alike.' So painfully alike! 'You *must* love Stacy enough to want her happiness . . .' she trailed off hopelessly, stunned by the ferocious glare in his eyes.

'Shall I tell you what I see when I look at Stacy, you little bitch?' he growled with rage, his face becoming a molten red. 'I see that picture of your father that Marie kept in the locket he gave her—the locket she never took off, while the jewellery I gave to her lay untouched in her jewellery box. I see her staring out at nothing with that beautiful, dreamy smile on her face, then turning and looking *through* me. I see her eyes moving compulsively over you, searching out every expression, every look that was his. Tell me now,' he sneered savagely, 'how much I must love Stacy.'

'You hate her, don't you?' Caroline whispered brokenly, finally understanding the extent of his twisted resentment. 'And you hated my mother . . .'

'Hated her, Caroline?' his mouth twisted with the words. 'No, I didn't hate her. I loved her, for years I loved her . . . It was your father I hated—everything he was, everything he did, everything he touched. Marie never let go of him. That bastard had everything I'd ever wanted. Even when he was dead, he still held on to everything I wanted.' He looked at her with bitter rage, inviting her to share the hurtful irony of his words.

Caroline couldn't bear any more. She could not let Stacy stay with this man . . . She brought her hands up to cover her face, pity and despair and contempt tightening her throat and forcing tears to her eyes. He had spent all these years, tortured, haunted by the ghost of her father. His hatred and jealousy had warped him, leaving him bleeding slow, deadly poison inside.

'And that ring!' Lawrence snarled, savagely twisting her left hand down from her face, his fingers biting into her flesh as he stared malevolently at the wedding ring on her finger. 'She never let it out of her sight. She knew she couldn't keep it after she married me, so she did the next best thing—she gave it to you, and it was always there. Her eyes were always on it. My God, how I hate the sight of that ring!' Lawrence's face contorted into a mask of dark menace, his eyes moving over Caroline with savage intent.

'You,' he hissed hoarsely, 'you, always reminding her of him!' He took a threatening step towards her, and Caroline took one back, a silent partner in their macabre dance.

Memories of other times crowded her brain, the same sick sensation curling in the pit of her stomach. The pain of scars that never healed and bruises that never faded seared in her mind.

'Not again,' she thought wildly. 'Please God, not again!' She turned in blind panic and ran out of the kitchen. If she could just get outside, get to one of the neighbours . . .

Lawrence snagged her halfway across the living room, his face livid with rage. He pulled her roughly to his body, his alcohol-laden breath nearly gagging her . . .

Barrett Rossiter's eyes quickly scanned the line of mailboxes, searching for Caroline's name. There it was—Apartment No. 206. Squaring his shoulders in a typical gesture of stark determination, he pushed the call button for the elevator with a vicious finger. He knew what he had to do, and he knew that Caroline wasn't going to make it easy for him. He had been in the wrong. That stricken look on her face as she had pulled away from him haunted him, but dammit all, it hadn't been his fault entirely. And she had responded in the beginning—unconsciously, maybe, but responded none the less. A hard shudder racked him as he remembered the softness of her lips and the warm, sweet feel of her skin against his.

Barrett pushed the memory away. He was here to apologise for what had happened, not to relive it.

He had no problem locating her apartment. Lifting his hand to knock on her door, he suddenly stopped. What if her husband was home? What would he do then? He ran a restless hand through his shining dark hair, mussing its ordered smoothness. How do you apologise to a woman for forcing yourself on her with her husband present? he wondered grimly. Dear God, he didn't even want to see the man, much less provoke him into a fight. Barrett was afraid of the opportunity it presented ... From the moment he had first seen that wedding ring on Caroline's finger, he had been aching to smash his fist into her husband's face. Somehow, it seemed if he never saw her husband, then he didn't exist. Simple, twisted logic, he told himself grimly. You ought to go and have your head examined. A reproving Freud-like tone floated through his mind. 'Ve vill have to keep your brain for a veek or so, dear fellow. Ja, Ja, you are quite insane.' Barrett smiled involuntarily. Caroline would agree. Caroline ...

A stubborn expression settled on his lean, dark face, his eyes hardening perceptibly. Once again he lifted his hand to knock, but this time was stilled by one soft whimper penetrating through the door and then the muffled sound of flesh meeting flesh in violent contact.

Barrett's hand was instantly at the doorknob, pushing forward into the room before he was aware of his actions. Nothing of the rather shabby surroundings registered in his mind. His eyes immediately found Caroline, cowering on the floor, an angry red mark on her cheekbone already turning into a painful bruise. A huge man stood over her prone form, his grizzled face contorted with fury, one calloused fist raised explicitly, ready to strike again.

Both faces turned to him as he crashed through the door. Two pairs of eyes took in the tense, muscled body and the fists clenching and unclenching by his sides. A white tension stiffened his jaw as the three of them seemed frozen for one unbearable moment in the curiously silent room.

Caroline broke the silence, her pain-filled eyes seeming glued to his face, sensing his rage and terrified by the coldness in his eyes.

'Barrett,' she croaked, blood trickling from the corner of her mouth.

That pitiful plea tightened something in him, tore at something inside him. He slowly pulled his eyes from her and turned to Lawrence with deadly menace.

Lawrence rounded on Barrett, words falling roughly from his ugly, slackened mouth. 'Listen here, sonny boy, I don't know who you——' he got no further. Barrett's fist shot out with an almost casual savagery, connecting squarely with Lawrence's jaw, causing him to reel back, stunned and bleeding. Barrett followed, icy-hot with rage. He sat out to methodically tear Lawrence apart, the fury frozen on his face. He pummelled him until he fell to his knees, unable to stand, then he dragged him up by his collar and the thrashing continued, and all the while, the curiously frozen mask of intent covered Barrett's face.

The memory of Caroline cowering on the floor, blood on her face, blinded Barrett to reason and reality. Neither the near-unconscious moans torn from Lawrence's swollen lips, nor Caroline's desperate pleas, could pierce the fury coursing through him.

Lawrence was hanging, unconscious, from Barrett's hands when Caroline's muffled sobs finally reached him. Her hands were clinging to his shoulders, her arms thrown around his back from behind in an effort to drag him away from the man dangling limply from his bleeding knuckles.

'Please, Barrett, please stop! You're going to kill him,' she moaned weakly.

Barrett turned to her, seeing the pathetic tears sliding down her face. He released his hold on Lawrence's shirt, throwing him to the floor as though the touch of him were repulsive. Lawrence landed with a thud, taking a table with him, and laid there, unmoving. Barrett's eyes never left Caroline's face, searching over each feature with scorching intensity, his jaw tense and his lips white with rage. The fire in him had not yet died.

His eyes finally came to rest on her swollen lips, and his fingers closely followed, running so lightly over the planes and hollows of her face that she almost didn't feel their butterfly touch. The silence was stark, filling the room, seeming to smother her in its vastness. That this man who had just destroyed her stepfather could turn to her one second later and display such heart-stopping gentleness amazed her. Having lived with her stepfather all those years had taught her much about violence, but nothing about the tenderness that sometimes causes it and goes with it. It was a revelation for her.

Barrett's fingers continued delicately tracing her swollen lips, his smoky eyes following the movement hypnotically, and Caroline half stifled a cry of pain. But it was a kind of pain she had never before experienced, a deep, hard ache centred in her breast.

Barrett drew a deep, ragged breath at the sound, his eyes darkening as he took a purposeful step towards the recumbent form on the floor.

'No, Barrett, please don't,' she pleaded softly, begging him to stop. 'He didn't hurt me.'

He froze and turned back to her, his eyes scanning her face once more and coming to rest on her mouth. 'You're bleeding,' he muttered with barely suppressed violence, his eyes taking on that blind fury that frightened Caroline so. 'This bastard——' he gave Lawrence a prodding kick with his foot, '——made you bleed. Why should I stop?' he demanded through tightly clenched teeth.

Caroline raised a shaky hand to her temple as though she was trying to soothe away the memory of what had happened.

'Because that bastard——' she finally answered wearily, 'is my stepfather.'

'Barrett's eyes narrowed in swift shock. 'I thought——'

'You thought——?' she prompted woodenly, not really caring, too frightened and tired and hurt to wonder.

'Never mind,' he dismissed quietly, noting the paleness of her skin.

'Please, just get him out of here. I hate the sight of him.' Her voice broke and she turned away, pressing trembling hands over her face. She was ashamed of her weakness, but those probing silvery eyes seemed to be dissecting her soul and she was frightened of what they might find.

Barrett turned away, hoisting Lawrence's not inconsiderable weight easily over one broad shoulder. As though he does this sort of thing often, Caroline thought wildly, hysteria setting in. Maybe he spends his free time listening at doors, hoping to find a damsel in distress. Tonight was my night. Aren't I lucky? Her fingers bit deeply into her arm, forcing her thoughts back to some semblance of sanity. God, aren't I lucky? she echoed grimly. How badly would Lawrence have beaten her this time if Barrett had not saved her? Lucky, she chanted soundlessly. Lucky, lucky, lucky.

Barrett hauled Lawrence down the corridor, stopping at the elevator. He pushed the call button and stared blankly at the wall, trying to think of nothing while he waited. When the elevator finally appeared, fortunately empty, he dumped Lawrence into the corner with careless disdain and pressed the button for the ground floor. Let someone else take care of the swine, he thought viciously, watching the doors close on the still form on the floor.

He quickly retraced his steps to Caroline's apartment. As he reached the door he heard her voice, its very urgency enough to stop him in his tracks. He was out of sight beyond the door, and he knew that she was not aware of his return. He strained to pick up her words, realising she was speaking on the phone. Caroline was talking very quickly and quietly, afraid of being overheard.

'Stacy, listen to me—this is important. I've just talked to Betty Clark. Her girls want you to spend the night with them. Would you like that?' A pause. 'Good. Mr Clark is on his way to pick you up. I know how much you like the girls, so you're sure to have a good time.' Caroline made a pathetic attempt at levity. The other party—Stacy—obviously asked a question, for there was a listening silence, then, 'No, honey, you don't have to leave a note for him. I just saw him. He's—not feeling well, so it's probably best if you aren't there tonight. He'll be better tomorrow and I'll take you——' here Caroline faltered, '—I'll take you back to him tomorrow.' Another pause. 'Oh, Stacy, I wish you could come too . . . No, I tried. I asked him, but he said no . . . Oh, Stacy, don't cry, please don't cry.' Caro's voice was rough with pain. 'We'll find a way, I promise. Then you can come and stay with me for ever, okay? Mr Clark is there? Put him on for a second, angel . . . Jim? You're sure it's okay for Stacy to stay with you? I'd take her myself, but he might be back . . . no, I'll be fine, don't worry about me. Please, just make sure she's safe. I'll be by to pick her up around six. And Jim . . . thank you.'

The faint sound of the receiver being replaced released Barrett from his silent vigil. An abrupt, muffled sob reached him, then another, compelling him across the room to Caroline's side.

She was seated on the couch, her head buried in her hands defeatedly, her shoulders shaking convulsively with sobs. She was crying as though her heart would break, and Barrett flinched from the soft, wounded sounds she was making. He knelt before her and, with exquisite gentleness, conscious of her bruises, gathered her into the warm circle of his arms.

'Sssh, baby,' he soothed huskily, rocking her gently in his arms, 'please don't cry like that. God, you're tearing me apart! You're going to make yourself ill. Ah, baby, sssh . . .' he crooned, his arms tightening consolingly around her.

Caroline's tears would not stop. She had not cried for a very long time, and now her misery and fear had taken control, breaking through the bonds of restraint she had imposed for so long. Yes, Stacy was safe for tonight; Jim and Betty Clark would see to that. But what about tomorrow when Caroline had to take her back to Lawrence? What about the next time Lawrence drank too much? Would she be safe with him? She could not bear the thought of Lawrence abusing Stacy the way he had abused her. She had to find a way to get custody of Stacy. She had to!

The burning determination of her thoughts gradually calmed her, and her sobs slowly subsided. Shaking, uneven breaths tore through her body even yet, as she fought to regain control.

Barrett turned her face up to his with an enquiring hand, searching her face with sober eyes. One strong finger smoothed down her cheek, following the gleaming wet trek of her tears.

'Okay?' he questioned huskily, one arm still curved protectively around her shuddering form.

Caroline nodded, subdued.

'We have to do something about this——' His finger flickered to her bottom lip, where the blood had now dried, and his eyes flamed dangerously.

Caroline recoiled from the wrath in his eyes, causing his lips to tighten as he felt her slight withdrawal.

'It's all right,' he murmured softly, one hand entwining in her tousled hair. 'I won't hurt you—I would never hurt you. Don't you know that?'

She gazed at him with the wide, wary eyes of a doe being hunted by unseen predators, unwilling to trust the very things that gave her life—the trees, the grasses, the bushes—for they also provided shelter for those who sought to hurt her.

Barrett shook his head as he read her eyes, trapped by the fear and the wariness he saw there as much as she was. His grey eyes stared past her, trying to ignore that hunted look, the silence thundering around them.

His eyes suddenly snapped back to her as he felt her small, cool hand tentatively steal over his jaw. Her eyes gleamed with a great hunger for security. Swinging her high into his arms and carrying her easily to her bedroom, he wondered bleakly if he had the right to offer the safety and warmth she so painfully craved.

He laid her tenderly in the middle of the bed and sat beside her, his eyes straining to see her face in the gathering gloom of the room, but his hand did not go out to the light by the bed.

Caroline stared up at him with dull eyes, the emptiness engulfing her. She was numb. One hour ago she had hated this man with a frightened passion, determined to erase all memory of him. Now he was her strength. Without him, she would crumble. She turned her head into her pillow and closed her eyes tightly, hopelessly trying to hold on to the numbness and deny the pain.

The bed shifted as Barrett's weight was removed, and Caroline turned her head in time to see him disappear into the adjoining bathroom.

He was back in a second, carrying a moist cloth in one hand. Again he seated himself on her bed, one hand bracing beside her as he gently dealt with the blood at the corner of her mouth. Finally, the heavy, dark silence was broken by his ragged, indrawn breath.

'Why was he beating you?' he questioned in a muffled tone, his smouldering eyes focused unblinkingly on her mouth. An involuntary shudder racked her body, and his eyes snapped up to meet hers, clouded with pain.

She turned her head away. 'I——' she stopped.

'You——?' he prompted quietly.

'He was drunk,' she murmured almost inaudibly. 'I don't want to talk about it. Please,' she pleaded, seeing the determined look tightening his face.

'All right,' he conceded reluctantly, his fingers lightly tracing the bruise along her cheekbone. 'No more questions.'

'Thank you,' she whispered tightly, feeling her skin

tauten as his fingers continued their idle wandering. Not just for——' she broke off, indicating the cloth he had used to wipe the blood from her lip where it lay on the dressing-table. 'Thank you for——' she stammered badly, '—for stopping him . . .'

A violent curse was torn from Barrett's throat.

'Honey . . .' he whispered, smoothing the long red-gold hair from her face, then moving downward to trace the swollen fullness of her lips with a compassionate finger. 'I'm so sorry this had to happen to you . . .' he husked.

Caroline knew she shouldn't, knew it was wrong, but she couldn't stop herself from catching his soothing fingers and pressing her lips to them in soft passion. She needed this man. She needed his calming words and his caressing hands. She needed his comfort and his warmth and his gentleness. She needed his strong, lean body and protective arms. And she longed for the feel, the taste of his lips.

Barrett's eyes narrowed dangerously as he felt her warm lips nuzzling his hand, his eyes darkening with the desire she had aroused with that one innocent touch. Slowly he bent to her, their eyes meeting and locking together in a hot, sweet message as old as time before her eyes fluttered closed, waiting for the inevitable touch of his lips.

She did not wait for long. His mouth moved on hers in a light, butterfly caress, testing and warming. A small moan forced its way past hungry lips and her eyes opened with sensual slowness. She made no attempt to guard her expression, her face alive with excitement and an almost unbearable longing.

What he read there seemed to reassure Barrett. His hands lifted to frame her face tenderly, his eyes moving over each feature, savouring the beauty and the unashamed desire shining there, seeking to brand each part of her into his mind and body.

Once again he bent to her, his mouth soothing lightly, kissing her lips but not joining with them, driving her wild with their deliberate teasing. Her hands locked behind his head, pulling him to her forcefully, urging his lips to claim hers. A long groan of defeat escaped him. His mouth took hers, but this time with a hot passion that left no room for doubts. His teeth nibbled at the soft underside of her bottom lip, a deliberate seduction that tensed her entire body to his command. The pain her split lip was causing mingled with the pleasure Barrett was instilling, until it was impossible to separate the two. She longed for both, knowing she would eagerly accept anything this man offered.

It felt so right, his lips moving caressingly over her face, his hands roaming over her body with a reverent worship that Caroline could not, did not want to deny. She flowed with the storming stream of desire that engulfed them, urging her body to his, a perfect half of the whole.

A soft rush of cool air poured over her heated skin as her blouse was eased from her shoulders with passionate impatience. Her bra quickly followed, releasing its surging burden to Barrett's arousing hands. Her nipples flowered beneath his teasing, probing fingers and she moaned in ecstasy.

Her hand tugged impatiently at his shirt, freeing it from his waistband and quickly releasing the buttons. Trembling hands pushed it from his shoulders, leaving his hair-roughened chest bare to her exploring hands. Her hands seemed to assume a will of their own, moving lower, deftly unsnapping the waistband of his pants, and she had no desire to stop them.

Her whole body was searching, straining to the thrusting hardness of his hips, which she knew, with sudden certainty, was the only satisfaction she would ever crave, the only guide she would ever allow to lead her to the warm security of a private paradise.

A heavy, smothering silence enveloped them, broken only by the harsh drag of their breathing and the strangled endearments torn from their throats.

Caroline's skirt had long since been removed, lying on the floor beside the bed. Barrett's hand passed from neck to thigh in long, arousing sweeps.

'Barrett!' she cried on a sharply indrawn breath, amazed and enraptured by the sensations he was creating with his knowing fingers.

'Caro! You're so beautiful . . . I want you. I want you so badly,' he whispered hoarsely, his mouth deserting its gentle sucking at her breast to catch hers in passionate demand. His leg was flung over both of hers, holding her still on the bed beneath him, trapping her to the hard demand of his body.

Her whole body was vibrating with tiny shudders of anticipation. She lifted her left hand, brushing a sweep of unruly dark hair away from his eyes, smiling with intimate acceptance.

'Take me, Barrett,' she begged unsteadily. 'Make me yours. And let me make you mine . . .'

Barrett was not proof against the aroused light shining in her eyes, and he moved to deepen their intimacy when suddenly his expression changed, his jaw tensing whitely as his eyes fixed unblinkingly on the finger that glittered with the wide gold symbol of another man's possession.

Terrified that he was going to leave her, deny her the satisfaction only he could give, Caroline clung to him, questioning his withdrawal in a shaking whisper. 'Barrett?'

Barrett's large hands once again moved to frame her face, studying her expression intently. His eyes were still glazed with passion, but something else, something she could not identify, mingled there. 'You realise how this will complicate everything for us? You understand what it will mean?' he demanded hoarsely.

'I don't care,' she denied feverishly. She only understood that she had to sate herself with his body, to satisfy his needs and in doing so, satisfy her own.

He read her face, etched with desperate need, his hands stroking lightly through her tousled hair.

'Dear God, why did you have to be married?' he ground out tightly, not waiting for an answer, not wanting one. He wasn't going to stop—he couldn't. The body beneath his was too warm, too inviting, flaming his passion out of control.

Caroline, her body writhing hungrily under his, demanding his possession, could not monitor her words.

'I'm not married, Barrett,' she blurted with burning impatience. 'The wedding ring—it's my mother's. I didn't think it mattered what you thought, but now . . .' Her hand clung weakly to his shoulder, the tense desire that tautened her jaw and squeezed her eyes shut blinding her to the wild rage and realisation sweeping over him.

'Please,' she moaned piteously, 'please make love to me.'

'Make love to you?' Barrett repeated numbly, as though he had never heard the words before. 'I ought to beat the hell out of you!' he roared, pulling her hands from his shoulders. Dragging himself from the bed, he paced the floor in darkness, his words cutting into her cruelly. 'Do you know what you did to me? Do you have any idea how the thought of you with another man—a husband—has eaten at me? You damn near emasculated me!' He stopped pacing to stare down at her gleaming body on the rumpled bed. 'Did you think you could make me want you so much that I'd overlook the lies, give you anything? Is that it? Or did you want me at all? Was it the money? Were you going to make me your lover, then threaten to tell your "husband" if I didn't pay up? Is that how you work your little game?' His eyes raked over her contemptuously. 'Why don't you just charge by the hour? It'd be a hell of a lot more honest!'

He began throwing on his clothes with careless haste, ignoring her stunned denials.

'I don't know what you're talking about. Barrett, please——'

'Save it, lady,' he cut in rudely, crossing the room. With one final, derisive survey he pushed open the door. 'No wonder he was beating you,' he sneered hurtfully. 'He should have done it before.'

'He did,' Caroline whispered dully, her throat working convulsively. Barrett did not hear. He had slammed out of the apartment and into the night.

Hours later, Barrett straightened behind the wheel of his car, ignoring the protest of his aching muscles and the stiffness of his neck. He looked blearily at his watch. Five-forty-five. It was beginning to get light. Caroline would be safe now; her stepfather had not returned. Barrett turned the ignition with a single flick of his wrist and slowly eased away from the kerb in front of Caroline's apartment building.

CHAPTER SIX

FOR Caroline, the night crept past, each second agonising. She did not sleep. She lay still and silent in her bed during the darkest hours of the night and on through the dusky warning of a new day. Her dull eyes gazed unblinkingly at the ceiling, her mind working with a curiously painful slowness, as she relived over and over again the events of the previous day . . . Her stepfather's contorted face, Barrett's passion, then later his fury, Stacy's trembling frightened voice—they all stormed through her mind, playing themselves out on the screen-like blankness of the ceiling.

Suddenly, the rude buzzing of her alarm broke the stillness of the room. She reached indifferently to silence it, but her eyes did not waver. It was as if she was watching a horror movie—she couldn't stand to see what was unfolding before her eyes, but somehow she could not force herself to turn from it, afraid of what she would find waiting for her beyond the darkness.

She didn't remember setting the alarm. After Barrett had left, after what had seemed like hours of emptiness and coldness, she had dragged herself from the crumpled bed and mechanically performed the night-time ritual of pulling on her robe and padding silently into the bathroom to wash and brush her teeth.

A white-faced, hollow-cheeked ghost with wildly glittering eyes had stared back at her from the mirror, mocking her every action. Caroline trembled when she finally realised that the ghost was her own reflection. She wanted to be angry at what her stepfather and Barrett had done to her, she wanted to hit out at them as they both had hit out at her, but during those long, bleak hours of the night, as she gazed unseeingly into the darkness, she could not find the spirit or the strength. They had robbed her of both.

Last night, the coupling of Barrett and Lawrence in her mind as 'they'—the assaulters, the thieves—had come naturally. In her mind, they had both abused her, deliberately and cold-bloodedly trampled the parts of her she had not been able to shelter. They were both takers, users, destroyers. The frightened, bruised part of her had tarred them with the same brush, hopelessly trying to fuse a knot of hatred and strength.

The rude light of morning cut softly through the subterfuge. Barrett had taken only what she had so willingly offered, used only what she had begged him to take. Caroline was the thief. She had tried to take something that was not—could never be—hers ... the sweet warmth of Barrett's body, and his love.

A bitter laugh escaped her. She could even understand the fury that had led to his rejection of her. He had only wanted a sweet, easy affair with a married woman, someone who would not cause trouble or make demands he was unwilling or unable to meet. A married woman, her tired brain reasoned, had too much to lose. Caroline pushed to the back of her mind the words torn from Barrett's throat in the heat of his passion. 'You realise how this will complicate everything for us.'

He had saved her from Lawrence's brutal hands—the realisation forced itself into her crowded brain. He had saved her. That was the bottom line.

Caroline slipped from the bed. She did not ever want to have to face Barrett Rossiter again, but she owed him for what he had done. She would go to the office, thank him for his help, and hand in her resignation. She doubted if he would insist that she work out a two-week notice. She would be free of Barrett.

No feeling of relief came with the thought. But it was necessary. She always paid her debts.

The offices that Caroline shared with Barrett were still, silent. No presence marred the awful yawning void engulfing the rooms. Caroline forced tense fingers to release their death grip on the doorknob, and pushed herself reluctantly into her office.

Barrett had not yet arrived. She drew a trembling, shallow breath. She had time to type her resignation.

One hour later, Barrett entered the room, striding briskly past her as she sat behind her desk, transcribing tapes from English to Spanish.

He looked haggard, his skin grey and taut, deep lines of exhaustion graven in his face. What did he do, where did he go after he left me last night? Caroline wondered painfully. Her jade eyes followed him hypnotically as he disappeared into his office and slammed the door behind him, fear and hunger mingled in their depths.

In the dark, empty hours of the night, Caroline had finally resolved her feelings for Barrett, and the final understanding was more painful than she had believed possible. The hurt cut more deeply into her than any punishment Lawrence had ever inflicted. It wasn't only sexual attraction that drew her to Barrett, and it wasn't only a need for the safety of his arms. Yes, both of those were part of the whole, but there was more, so much more ... respect and desire and liking and affection, and the recognition of the other half of herself. The whole was love. She loved Barrett, without qualms, without reservations. He excited her, and frightened her, his touch could comfort or arouse, his smile soothe or punish. He was her weakness and her strength. And loving him was tearing her apart, because she knew that her love would never be returned. There was too much between them now to ever start again. It was this knowledge that made Caroline crumble. How could she live without him now? she asked herself dully. Dear God, how could she leave now?

But leave she must.

'Caroline!' Barrett roared, her resignation clutched in one strong hand, his fingers slowly crushing it into a ball.

Caroline rushed through the communicating door, stopping short as she registered the angry set of his mouth.

'What——' Barrett questioned in a dangerously quiet tone, throwing the crumpled paper at her feet, '—is this?'

She swallowed grimly, pride stiffening her spine. 'My resignation,' she answered flatly meeting his eyes without flinching.

'Your resignation,' he echoed softly. 'Perhaps you'd care to elaborate.'

'I'm leaving. I can't——' her voice broke for one brief second and the level grey eyes sharpened. 'I don't want to work for you any more.'

'You don't want to work for me any more,' Barrett repeated slowly, the cold menace in his eyes sending a shiver down Caroline's spine: 'Why?'

She remained silent. How could she answer that? Because I love you, and I can't bear to live with your dislike and contempt, day after day, her heart screamed. Because being near you and not touching you requires more strength than I'll ever have.

'It can't be because of our little—scene—last night,' Barrett scoffed, breaking in on her tortured thoughts. 'Are you so upset that you were found out?'

'You—you don't believe that.' Her eyes were agonised.

'Don't I?' Barrett derided harshly. 'I thought I did.'

'It's not true . . .'

'Then why, Caroline?' he probed ruthlessly. 'Why the lies, why the games?'

'I didn't . . . lie!' she denied heatedly. 'I never told anyone that I was married. It was Ronald Waxler who did that.'

'But you played along.'

'Yes, I played along! He wasn't going to give me the job because I was a woman, but when he saw the wedding ring . . .' she fingered it defensively as Barrett's eyes narrowed malevolently on the gold band, '. . . he

seemed to think it would be all right to give me the job
if I was married——'

'Ah yes, the wedding ring ... tell me about the
wedding ring, Caroline,' Barrett invited softly. 'Why
were you wearing it, in the first place, if not with the
intention of deceiving?'

'I told you, it was my—mother's.' Grief formed a
painful lump in her throat as she choked out the
explanation. 'She ... she gave it to me, after my father
died ... after she married—Lawrence.'

Barrett's jaw tensed whitely at the name.

'You had no right to make married status a condition
of employment,' Caroline attacked bitterly. 'You had
no right!'

'And what right did you have to lie about that
marital status?'

'I didn't lie!' she protested hotly.

'You lied with your silence,' Barrett condemned
flatly. 'Did you want the job so badly that you would
lie to get it, Caroline?'

Her head lifted proudly. 'Yes,' she admitted simply. 'I
would have done anything to get this job.'

'Anything?' he echoed with cynically raised brows.
'Perhaps I needn't have walked out on you last night,'
he said cruelly.

Caroline flushed painfully, but said nothing, unable
to deny, even to herself her response to him last night.
But he must never know that response was prompted
by love. Surely she could be spared that humiliation, if
nothing else.

'Why, Caroline?' Barrett demanded, his tone gentling
in the face of her weary resignation. 'Why was this job
so important to you? So important that you would even
sleep with me to keep it?'

She drew a harsh breath, but said nothing. It was
better to let Barrett think her only reason for inviting
his lovemaking was her desire to keep her job.

'Why, Caroline?'

'I ... needed the money,' she evaded.

'Why did you need the money?'

She shifted restlessly, avoiding his dissecting eyes. 'Everybody—everybody needs money,' she supplied finally.

The flat of Barrett's palm met his desk in violent contact, the sharp retort reverberating around the walls and snapping her wide eyes to his furious face.

'Damn you, Caroline, I'm tired of your evasions! Answer my question. Why did you need the money?'

'It's none of your business!' she flared. 'You've got my resignation—I'm leaving. Isn't that enough for you?'

'No,' Barrett answered in an odd, grim tone, 'it's not enough. It will never be enough.' Then, brusquely, 'I know all this has something to do with your worthless stepfather—I've worked that much out. What is it, Caroline?' he pressed urgently. 'Tell me—talk to me. I can help you.'

'No,' Caroline denied, 'you can't help. Nobody can help. This is between myself and Lawrence and Sta——' She stopped abruptly, realising that she had almost blurted out Stacy's name. Barrett was not stupid. He would push until he found all the answers he was looking for if she was weak enough to drop unconscious clues.

Barrett pounced. 'Between you and Lawrence and—who, Caroline?' Then, suddenly remembering the conversation he had overheard last night after he had dumped Lawrence in the elevator, he moved in for the kill. 'Between you and Lawrence and *Stacy*, Caroline? Is that what you were about to say?'

Caroline's guilty start was an admission in itself.

'Who is Stacy, Caroline?'

She said nothing, her eyes fixed determinedly on her tense fingers.

Impatient with her stubborn refusal to speak, Barrett began to unravel the puzzle himself.

'You told her to spend the night with "the girls". You arranged to have someone pick her up and keep her until this evening . . .'

'You listened!' Caroline spluttered indignantly. 'You——'

Barrett ignored her outburst completely.

'A little girl, I'd say. Living with your stepfather. Someone you love,' he speculated thoughtfully. 'Your—daughter?'

'My sister,' Caroline corrected tightly.

'Ah,' he breathed in comprehension. 'Tell me.'

Her shoulders slumped. She was beaten. He would find out one way or another, she knew, and it would be such a relief to talk to someone about Stacy, bittersweet ecstasy to share something with Barrett.

She walked past his desk, careful to avoid any contact with his body, and to the window, to stare out blindly. She felt his eyes studying her intently.

'My mother married Lawrence Redden six years ago,' she began tightly, not even aware of the whiteness of her knuckles as she clenched her hands to prevent a visible tremor or the pinched tenseness around her lips. 'My father had just died. I was sixteen, Stacy just a baby. My parents loved each other very much. When Dad died, it was as if Mom died with him. I couldn't . . . reach her any more,' Caroline revealed sadly, lost in the empty days following her father's death. 'She just sat for endless hours in their room, alone. I tried to help,' she mumbled hopelessly. 'I took care of Stacy, and I made sure Mom ate, but it wasn't enough. I couldn't—couldn't bring Mom back to us.

'Gradually, as time went by, Mom pulled out of her darkness enough to realise that we couldn't go on like we were. The insurance money was running out. Mom had two children to support, and no way of doing it. And—Lawrence was there. She didn't care about herself any more. I honestly think she spent the last six years of her life marking time until she could be with my dad again . . .' Caroline's words were wistfully grave, darkly sombre as she relived those lost days.

'Mom married Lawrence . . . to give us a "stable" home life, she said.' Caroline's mouth twisted bitterly.

'And instead Redden beat you,' Barrett finished grimly.

She shook her head. 'Not—not until after Mom died six months ago,' she corrected tautly. 'And never the way he was going to ... last night. It was al—always just ... bruises.' Barrett shifted sharply and she hurried on, 'Oh, he always threatened—that's how he kept Mom in line, through Stacy and me, but after Mom died, something ... snapped. He started to drink more and more ... It gave him courage, I think.

'He "loved" her,' she revealed gratingly. 'That was one thing he told me last night before ... But his love was so twisted, so warped! And when he finally realised that Mom could never love him in return, it turned to poison ... it ate him up ...'

'Why didn't you just take Stacy and leave when your mother died?' Barrett demanded roughly, his long body tense with anger.

Caroline stiffened at the condemning tone. 'He has custody of Stacy. But he promised me that when I got a job, when I could provide a stable home, he would give me custody.'

'That's why you needed this job so badly,' he stated wearily.

'Yes.' She swallowed the tightness in her throat. 'But last night—he told told me he'd changed his mind, that he wasn't going to let me have Stacy ... God, I hate him!' Caroline trembled with the force of the emotions warring inside of her. 'He does it to hurt me, refusing to let me have custody——'

'Does he beat Stacy?' Barrett asked grimly.

'No!' she denied harshly. 'Do you honestly think I would have let her stay with him all this time if he did? I would have taken her away, no matter what he did to me——'

'Why you? Why does he beat you?' The question was savagely drawn.

'I—my father—I look like him. And the ring ...' she gestured vaguely with her hand. 'He said my mother gave it to me so it would always ... be with her. So Dad would always be with her,' she managed the explanation with difficulty.

'So what are you going to do now?' Barrett pressed hardly. 'You're quitting your job. Tonight you're going to take an innocent child back to that twisted maniac— and you have no guarantees that he won't hurt her, or you, or both. He's going to be as mad as hell about what I did to him last night, and the two of you are the obvious targets——'

'Please! I don't know what to do,' Caroline moaned pitifully, tears rolling unchecked down her ashen cheeks. 'I don't know ...'

'Then I'll tell you, shall I?' he offered, rising at last and moving behind her, placing his hands on her quivering shoulders and drawing her resisting body against his. 'You'll marry me, and let me deal with it.'

Caroline went ramrod-stiff.

'M-marry you?' she repeated threadily. 'I don't—I don't ...'

Barrett's mouth was grim. 'Just listen,' he instructed shortly. 'I can help you win custody of your sister—I have the money and the contacts. But if I just give you the money, your stepfather will find some way to use it against you in the custody battle. He'll have the judge label you as my mistress, an unfit guardian.'

Caroline shuddered at the softly spoken words, and Barrett, pressed close against her back, felt the vibrations.

'But,' he continued more gently, 'if I were your husband, not only would you have the money to fight for custody, but you'd also have a good home and stable family life to offer Stacy. And by Stacy, I mean the judge, if it comes to that. Do you understand?'

'But—I ... I don't want to marry anybody!' Caroline shuddered. 'I'll never subject myself to the anguish my mother suffered for six long years ...'

'Not all marriages are like your mother's and your stepfather's,' Barrett spoke soothingly, his hands caressing her body calmingly. 'You said your parents were happy.'

'Don't you understand?' Caroline rounded on him frustratedly. 'That was the biggest part of her torment. To lose my father was the ultimate punishment. I saw what that did to her, and I never want to be placed in that position. Never!'

'Afraid to love, Caroline?' Barrett asked steadily.

'Afraid to love like that,' she admitted, her voice trembling.

'Your experience of marriage has been rather extreme,' he said carefully. 'One based on love, the other twisted into hatred.'

'And our marriage—what would it be based on?' Caroline voiced the question whose answer she feared most.

There was a thick pause before Barrett finally answered. 'Need. You need me, Caroline.'

She could not deny the truth of that statement. She needed him in so many different ways she didn't know where one stopped and another began. 'And you,' she asked shakily, 'what do you get out of this?'

Barrett's hands framed her face, his flaming eyes steady on hers.

'I get you,' he answered deliberately.

'It's not enough!' she protested weakly.

'It's a middle ground, Caroline,' Barrett said flatly. 'And it's all we have. I want you, I intend to have you. This way neither of us loses.'

Caroline pulled herself from his restraining arms. He was wrong, she wanted to scream at him. *She* would lose. She would lose every time he took her without love, every time his restless eyes rested on another woman. She would lose when he finally tired of her and walked away. But she would never be free of the love she felt, even when Barrett was free of her.

'I can't,' she whispered painfully. 'I can't.'

Barrett tensed behind her.

'Does Stacy mean so little to you, then?' he sneered

deliberately, 'that you think of yourself before her? Some "love"!'

Caroline whirled to face him, tears blurring her eyes. 'No, you're wrong! I love Stacy! I'd do anything for her.'

'Anything except take the one step that would insure she never has to go through the hell you went through! How long do you think it will be, Caroline, before your stepfather begins to beat her? A month? Two?' he hammered the point relentlessly. 'Maybe even a couple of years. By then Stacy will be ten, eleven. Yes,' he considered cruelly, 'I suppose that's as good an age as any to begin abusing a child . . .'

'Stop it! Oh God, Barrett, stop it!' Caroline begged hoarsely, her ashen face streaked with wild tears. She raised trembling hands to cover her ears, as though by doing this she could block out his words and the fears they aroused.

It was true, she realised in shaking terror. It was all true. Some day Lawrence's bitter rage would be turned on Stacy, and she would be destroyed by the twisted hatred that drove him, the depths of which Caroline had only begun to understand the night before. She couldn't, she couldn't let that happen to Stacy!

'You have no choice, Caroline,' Barrett said quietly, now sure of his victory. 'You know you're going to marry me.'

'I—yes.' The muffled admission was dragged from her lips. She would marry him. Like he said, she had no choice. But what refined torture it would be, married to Barrett, loving him, sharing his bed, but not his life, or his heart. It would destroy her, as surely as Lawrence's brutal hands would destroy Stacy if she did not marry Barrett. She had been forced to choose between saving Stacy and saving herself, and she had chosen Stacy.

Gentle hands cupped her face, raising her eyes to meet his sombre expression.

'It won't be so bad, you know,' he told her whimsically. 'You didn't mind too much last night——'

'Please, don't ...' Caroline murmured, shifting uncomfortably beneath his hands.

'Oh, but I will, Caroline,' he assured her explicitly. 'Any time and anywhere I want to. And I'll make you want it, too ...'

And that, Caroline realised fearfully, was what she was afraid of.

Barrett's lips began to explore the delicate hollows of her neck, nuzzling at the frantic pulse he found. The warm exploration continued as those tormenting lips trailed along the tense line of her jaw, his tongue delicately slipping over the soft, creamy skin, tasting her sweet warmth.

She trembled beneath the seductive onslaught. She had to stop him, she had to stop him now, or she would be lost.

'What about Stacy?' she breathed weakly, her voice a mere thread of sound.

Barrett's mouth stilled momentarily. 'What about Stacy?' he demanded with passionate impatience against her skin.

'I—I want custody as soon as possible. I don't want to take her back to ... him tonight,' Caroline spelled out stiltedly.

The allusion to Lawrence snapped Barrett back to the problem at hand instantly. 'You won't,' he promised, his tone steely. 'Neither you nor Stacy will ever have to see him again.'

Holding her eyes locked with his, Barrett moved to the telephone on his desk, and viciously punched out a series of numbers.

'Bennett, get up here now!' he barked into the receiver, not bothering with preliminaries, and slammed it down just as abruptly.

Bennett Durston was one of the lawyers who made up the Organisation's intimidating legal department. He was also a friend of Barrett's. They had been at school together, and Barrett knew he could rely on Ben's discretion.

An uneasy silence hovered between them as they waited for Ben Durston's arrival. Barrett did not try to touch her again, instead, he seated himself behind his desk while Caroline remained awkwardly standing in front of its polished surface. She was uncomfortably aware of the speculative cloudy eyes as they studied her minutely, but she refused to meet their silent challenge.

Ben Durston's arrival shifted Barrett's attention away from her, and she breathed an unsteady sigh of relief. The lawyer was thirty-three the same as Barrett, but already he had developed a slight paunch from too many extended lunch breaks, and too many hours behind a desk. His dark hair was a little too long to be fashionable or conservative, but his brown eyes, behind thick lenses, snapped with a keen intelligence. Not exciting, Caroline deduced silently, but trustworthy.

Barrett did not waste time on unnecessary niceties.

'We need a custody agreement drawn up,' he stated bluntly.

Ben's eyebrows rose dramatically. He turned to Caroline, his eyes moving swiftly over her body in a fair imitation of Sherlock Holmes searching for clues. Turning back to Barrett, he asked expressionlessly, 'When is it due?'

Caroline ground her teeth audibly.

'Try again, Mr Durston,' she ordered coldly.

Ben was taken aback. 'I'm sorry,' he apologised clumsily. 'I just assumed——'

'Don't assume, Ben,' Barrett cut in harshly. 'We haven't reached that point—yet.'

Again Ben's eyebrows rose, and Caroline clenched her fists tightly, aching to ram them into Barrett's cynical mouth.

'The agreement involves Caroline's little sister, who is currently in the custody of her stepfather,' Barrett informed the lawyer smoothly.

Ben nodded, snaring a pad and pen from Barrett's desk. 'Okay,' he prompted, turning to Caroline. 'Sister's name?'

'Stacy Marie Forsythe.'

'Stepfather's?'

'Lawrence Allen Redden.'

'Your full name?'

'Caroline Leigh Forsythe.'

Ben turned back to Barrett, the information neatly recorded on the pad he held. 'Shoot,' he instructed, pen poised.

'The terms are to be as follows,' Barrett dictated, leaning back in his chair. 'Redden will give up all custody claims on Stacy. Said custody will be turned over solely and completely to Caroline. There will be no support payments, no visitation rights. No contact between him and Caroline or Stacy, or legal action will be taken.'

Ben whistled. 'That's pretty rough——' he began.

'He's an alcoholic,' Barrett cut in coldly, his eyes moving to Caroline's bruised face, '——and brutal.'

Ben nodded peaceably, not missing the dark discolouration that marred Caroline's skin.

'There will be a further stipulation,' Barrett continued relentlessly, 'providing that in the event Caroline and I do not, for whatever reason, marry within the next ten days, custody will immediately revert back to Redden.' His eyes silvered in cold triumph as he played his trump, and Ben's head shot up disbelievingly. Caroline drew a sharp, angry breath.

'Barrett, you know——' Ben began protestingly, before Caroline's precise, stiff voice broke in.

'This isn't necessary, Barrett. I will not back out of our bargain.'

Barrett eyed her complacently.

'Let's just say I like to cover all my bases.'

Caroline turned on her heel and left the room without a single word.

As the door closed behind her, Ben turned to Barrett. 'You're crazy,' he muttered. 'You know that last stipulation is completely impossible—from a moral standpoint as well as a legal one. It's a blatant blackmail tactic——'

'It's the only hold I have,' Barrett interrupted, his words dangerously soft. 'Put it in.'

'I can't. She could use it against you later, if a divorce ensued——'

'There will be no divorce.' The words were formed in a cold hard statement of fact and thrown out like daggers. 'Put it in.'

Ben tried again. 'She could use it to have the marriage annulled.'

Barrett stiffened. 'How?'

'It's a pretty obvious indication that she's being forced to marry you, that you're exerting emotional blackmail. Marriage is a contract like any other. It is not valid if entered into under duress by either party,' Ben explained simply.

'All right,' Barrett conceded. 'Forget it. As long as she's convinced that she's not going to get Stacy without taking me, too . . .'

Ben shook his head dazedly. 'I never thought you'd have to force a woman to marry you, Barrett.'

'Just do it, Ben,' he ordered tightly. 'And then forget about it. This is not to go any farther than this room.'

'All right, ol' buddy, I'll do it. But you're still going to have to get Redden's signature on that custody release. How will you do it?'

Barrett's face hardened perceptibly. 'He'll sign it,' he promised darkly. 'Oh yes, he'll sign it.'

Barrett left the office exactly two minutes after Ben Durston's secretary delivered the typed custody agreement. Just long enough to read through it, Caroline surmised grimly. A curt, 'I'll be gone and hour or so,' preceded his exit from the office, an Caroline knew, with a shivering certainty, that he was going to confront Lawrence.

Barrett pounded on the door loudly, and stood tensely, waiting, listening to the echoing silence that answered his impatient summons. He lifted his hand again, the flat of his palm striking the wood of the door with determined insistence.

'All right, all right!' a hoarse, thick voice called finally through the door. 'No need to knock the damn door in . . .' the petulant words continued as the door was yanked open '. . . and I don't want anything!'

Lawrence Redden blocked the doorway pugnaciously, his thick body covered only by a dirty white undershirt and a pair of crumpled boxer shorts incongruously decorated with hearts and flowers. He peered at Barrett through bleary eyes, one of which was beautifully black and swollen almost completely shut. His hair stood in dirty spiked peaks, and a day's growth of beard shadowed his face, adding to the dissolute, unkempt appearance.

'Go 'way,' he muttered roughly through the pain of a split lip, turning away.

Barrett's mouth curled in contempt. 'Not so fast, Redden.' His harsh tone halted the other man's progress.

Lawrence turned back painfully, wincing at the sharp stab of agony from his bruised ribs.

'Do I know you?' he muttered vaguely, his eyes trying unsuccessfully to focus on the face of the man before him. 'Don't know you . . . go away,' he concluded gruffly.

'Take a closer look,' Barrett advised softly. Then, his gaze shifting to Lawrence's swollen eye, 'if you can,' he finished in malicious satisfaction.

'What the hell . . .?' Lawrence began, only to be interrupted as Barrett pushed past him, impatiently entering the house.

'We have something to discuss,' Barrett said threateningly, watching as Lawrence spun to confront him, then yelped from the pain of his action.

'Who are you, and what the *hell* do we have to discuss?' Lawrence blustered.

'My name is Barrett Rossiter. We met last night—in Caroline's apartment,' he spelled out clearly, deciding

Redden would probably never recognise him without prompting.

'You!' Lawrence growled menacingly. 'It was you who ...' One beefy finger raised to his black eye, indicating the visible evidence of the previous night's thrashing. 'I'm going to——'

'Save it,' Barrett advised curtly. 'I'm not impressed.'

'Was little Caroline impressed by your big man macho act last night?' Lawrence sneered nastily.

Barrett's face became a hard, dark mask. 'And what the hell would *you* know about being a man?' he asked derisively.

Lawrence ignored the question, studying Barrett suspiciously. 'What do you want?'

Barrett examined the cold, cheerless room unhurriedly, noting the worn, cheap furniture and the ragged, stained carpet, before turning back to Lawrence.

'I came to issue a friendly warning. Caroline and I are going to be married——'

'My, my,' Lawrence cut in uglily, 'she *was* impressed by your—performance last night, wasn't she?'

Barrett pinned him with a steely glance. 'Don't tempt me, Redden,' he warned softly, his eyes savagely cold. 'I'd love to repeat the lesson.'

Lawrence took two very careful steps backward, and Barrett's mouth twisted sardonically.

'We intend to have custody of Stacy,' he stated flatly.

'Stacy is in my custody. I won't give her up.'

'Don't be a fool,' Barrett derided curtly. 'You know and I know that any court in this state would take her away the second a suit was filed. You're an alcoholic, a child abuser, and——' he paused, his eyes contemptuous, '—a first-class bastard.'

Lawrence's face became a blotched red at the calculated insult.

'Don't push your luck, sonny boy,' he snarled. 'I've given you this much time because I sense a possibility of—compensation, shall we say?—but if you think——'

'Are you offering to sell me a seven-year-old girl?' Bennett disgustedly demanded clarification.

Lawrence's shrug was elaborately casual. 'We're both men of the world——'

'I've never been in your world, Redden,' Bennett snarled distastefully.

'—and as you said, I'd lose custody in a court battle,' Lawrence continued determinedly. 'I might as well get something out of it.'

'I suppose so,' Barrett agreed thoughtfully. 'What do you consider fair?'

An avaricious gleam brightened Lawrence's small bleary eyes.

'Ten thousand,' he answered greedily, measuring the impeccable cut of Barrett's suit, the dull gleam of gold at the cuffs of his shirt.

'What a bargain!' Barrett marvelled loathingly. 'No, Redden, I've got a better idea. You sign over custody of Stacy ... and I won't prosecute.'

Lawrence blanched. 'P-prosecute? What are you talking about?'

'Negotiating to sell a child, neglect, assault ... I think I could manage to have you locked away for a good many years. I have the money and the power to do it,' Bennett warned, flint-like, his tone deadly. 'Don't make the mistake of thinking I won't use it.'

'Five thousand,' Lawrence tried desperately.

A raw sound was torn from Barrett's throat. 'You——'

'Call it a payment for goods received,' Lawrence suggested. 'After all, Caroline is a piece of prime merchandise. I'm giving you what I had a yen to sample myself——' the words broke off abruptly as Barrett's hand shot out and clutched around Lawrence's thick neck.

'You bastard,' he enunciated coldly, his hand tightening. 'If you so much as *think* about touching Caroline, I'll take you apart piece by slimy piece. And next time——' he promised intently, '—I won't stop.'

'. . . can't breathe . . .' Lawrence gasped, his face tinged with blue.

Barrett threw him away in disgust.

'Choose.'

Lawrence held both hands to his neck. 'Take her, then,' he rasped viciously. 'I don't want the little brat anyway. Looks just like her mother—always whining——'

Barrett pulled the custody agreement from his suit pocket and threw it on the table before him.

'Sign it,' he ordered softly, holding out a pen.

Lawrence grabbed the pen roughly and scrawled his name angrily on the line provided at the bottom of the form.

'You've got both of them now,' he snarled, 'but don't come crawling to me when you want to get rid of them, because I won't take them back!'

Barrett picked up the form and folded it, his fingers closing around it securely.

'Just remember what I said,' he advised, crossing to the door. 'If you even get near either of them again, I'll make you wish you'd never been born!'

'I already do,' Lawrence muttered in glazed self-pity.

Barrett shut the door on the words.

Exactly fifty-three minutes after Barrett had left the office, he returned, casually tossing the signed agreement on Caroline's desk.

'My part of the deal,' he said quietly, his eyes careful.

She stared fixedly at the signature at the bottom of the document. He had signed it. Stacy was hers.

'How——?' she began bewilderedly.

Barrett's mouth twisted enigmatically. 'I asked nicely,' he said, walking to his office door. 'We'll pick up Stacy together.'

'But——'

'We'll leave at five.' Barrett nodded sharply. 'Be ready.'

And with that, Caroline thought weakly, as the office

door closed between them, she would have to be satisfied.

Caroline sat tensely, pressed painfully against the passenger door of Barrett's sleek black Jaguar, as they drove towards the Clarks' home. Her hands were tightly clenched in her lap.

'Scared?' Barrett questioned idly.

Caroline flashed him a quick, nervous glance.

'Yes,' she admitted shakily. 'There's so much at stake, so much to lose . . .'

'Except we aren't going to lose anything, Caroline,' Barrett promised firmly, reaching out to cover her twisting hands with one of his own.

She drew in a quick, shallow breath and jerked her hands from his, watching as his mouth tightened grimly at the reaction.

'I—I don't understand how you persuaded Lawrence to give up custody of Stacy without a fight?' Caroline rushed into speech, alarmed at the intent darkening of his eyes.

'You're going to have to do better than that, Caroline,' Barrett informed her silkily. 'Private resistance I can overcome,' he continued, supremely confident, 'but I will not have you acting as though my touch were repulsive. We both know better.'

Caroline said nothing, her glazed eyes fixed determinedly on the passing scenery. Repulsive! If he knew, she thought despairingly. She had pulled away from his hand, fearful of the fire his touch ignited. What would he say if he discovered the truth . . .

'As to Lawrence,' Barrett's dark tone, filled with distaste as he spoke of her stepfather, broke into her thoughts, 'we came to a—mutual understanding.'

'But how——?'

'It doesn't matter how,' Barrett silenced her. 'All that matters is that you need never worry about him again. Concentrate on Stacy—and me,' he finished deliberately.

'I hope—I hope Stacy likes you,' Caroline rushed in

nervously, wetting suddenly dry lips with the tip of her tongue.

He turned to her as he brought the car to a smooth stop in front of the Clarks' home. 'Well, we're——' his words broke off abruptly as his eyes focused and narrowed on Caroline's lips, and the pink tip of her tongue as it probed their surface.

She blushed fiercely at the leaping lick of desire flaming in his grey eyes, and drew her tongue in, pressing her lips together firmly.

'I——' Her words ceased jerkily as Barrett's hands cupped her face and drew her to him, his eyes fixed hungrily on her lips. When there remained only a breath of space separating their lips, Barrett's eyes flashed to hers, a gnawing question in their depths. Caroline answered in silent helplessness, unable to deny him—or herself.

His thumbs gently soothing along her jawline, he held her mouth poised for his pleasure. Once again his eyes lowered to her mouth, darkening at the parted invitation.

Slowly he bent his head, and a deep shuddering sigh racked her as she felt the delicate, hungry movement of his lips on hers. Caroline's hands lifted mechanically to his head, fingers threading longingly through the crisp black hair and down, to toy with the strong brown neck as Barrett continued the tasting exploration of her lips. Her whole body melted against him in unquestioning, unconditional surrender. Barrett's hands tensed on her jaw, ready to pull her to him and consolidate his victory. An urgent moan wrung from her throat, a silky kitten sound demanding satisfaction.

The sound seemed to jerk Barrett back into reality. He tore his hands from her, turning back to grip the steering wheel whitely. His harsh, rapid breathing ripped through the smothering silence his rejection had left behind.

'I think we should go see Stacy,' he grated roughly.

Caroline's eyes closed at his tone. Trembling hands

lifted to cover her tender lips. She didn't want to see Stacy, she screamed silently. She wanted to stay here, in his arms, to feel the touch of his lips on hers. But the hard, determined set of his mouth proclaimed a silent denial.

'I—yes,' she finally managed to agree in husky defeat. 'Let's go see Stacy.'

Barrett turned as she began to fumble with the door handle, his darkly disturbed eyes easily reading the hurt in her white face.

'Dammit all, Caro!' he swore wearily, running an agitated hand through his shining dark hair. 'I——'

'Please!' she stopped him. 'I—I don't want to talk about it. Let's just go.'

A tired sigh escaped him.

'Oh, we'll talk about it, Caroline,' he warned huskily. 'But not now. Not here.'

With those words still hanging on the air between them, he pushed out of the car, striding briskly around the front to help her alight. He slammed the door with leashed violence, then grasping her hand firmly in his, he walked to the Clarks' door and rapped peremptorily.

The sight that greeted Betty Clark as she opened the front door of her home was, to say the least, unexpected. Standing on the front porch, looking like a lost and bewildered child, stood Caroline Forsythe, her small hand completely lost in the grasp of the huge man looming protectively beside her.

'Hello, Betty.' Caroline was the first to speak, a forced smile plastered on her lips.

Not such a child, after all, Betty amended, her shrewd brown eyes noting the wild glittering need that had not yet died from Caroline's beautiful jade eyes, and the swollen peaks of her full breasts. Embarrassed, Betty transferred her curious gaze to the man's face, searching for signs of equal arousal and finding precisely nothing. The hard face was closed, no glimmer of emotion showing through. Maybe the answer she sought was to be found in the very lack of emotion etched in that ruggedly handsome face, Betty thought perceptively. No one could live for ever behind the mask this man was wearing.

Satisfied with her conclusions, Betty opened the door wide, inviting the couple in.

'Is Stacy all right?' Caroline asked urgently.

Compassion gleamed in Betty's warm brown eyes. 'She's fine, Caroline—honestly. The girls were up until midnight, giggling and playing.'

'She—she didn't say anything about—Lawrence?' Caroline persisted reluctantly.

'No.'

Betty and Jim Clark knew the state of affairs between Caroline and Lawrence, knew about his drinking. They were good friends, always willing to take Stacy on at a moment's notice. And Caroline, though an intensely private person, felt she owed them some kind of explanation. She told them as much as she could, but never did she breathe a word about his abuse of her. If Betty and Jim had their own suspicions, they tactfully refrained from voicing them.

'Where is she?' Caroline asked quietly.

'In the back yard, playing on the swing. Jim took the girls for a walk—we thought you might want to see her alone.' Betty explained calmly, not by a flicker of an eyelash revealing her curiosity about the stranger still holding Caroline's hand.

'Yes,' Caroline agreed distractedly, a faintly desperate look in her eyes, 'I have to talk to her alone . . .'

She glanced questioningly up at Barrett, seeking an answer to an unasked question.

Barrett understood. 'Go,' he advised quietly. 'Tell her. I'll be out in five minutes.'

Caroline nodded faintly and moved away, making her way to the back door.

Neither Betty nor Barrett said anything until they heard the almost silent closing of the door as it latched. Barrett turned to Betty, a rueful smile on his long mouth as he introduced himself.

'We never got around to introductions.' A hard smile laced the words. 'I'm Barrett Rossiter.'

'Betty Clark,' she reciprocated easily, wondering still at his presence.

'I'm Caroline's fiancé,' he added steadily.

'Oh!' Betty breathed in shock. 'I didn't realise—I didn't know Caroline was engaged.'

A wall seemed to go up behind Barrett's eyes. 'It's recent,' he told her quietly.

'When will you be married?'

'Next Friday,' he answered uncompromisingly.

'And Stacy——?' Betty probed worriedly.

'—will come to us.'

Realisation dawned. 'I see,' she murmured thoughtfully.

Barrett, reading the swift, disapproving understanding in her eyes, knew there was nothing left to say.

In the back yard, Stacy had just spotted Caroline.

'Carly!' she cried, hurling herself off the swing and into Caroline's waiting arms. 'Oh, Carly, it seems like I've been waiting for ever an' ever! I didn't think you was gonna come.'

'Stacy, you knew I'd come,' Caroline chided softly, tightening her hold protectively.

Stacy pulled away to look into Caroline's eyes, as always searching for the love she saw there. Her own blue eyes widened as she saw the angry bruise darkening her sister's cheek. A dirty, stubby finger lifted to trace it gently.

'He hurt you again, didn't he, Carly?' she asked in a trembling voice.

'Oh, Stacy,' Caroline's eyes closed briefly in pain, 'he'll never be able to hurt me, not really—I told you that.'

'But——' Stacy's young mind was not ready to accept such a denial.

'Listen, Stacy,' Caroline cut in gripping Stacy's hand between her own, 'I've got something to tell you.'

Stacy's eyes shadowed warily, and she squared her

thin shoulders determinedly. 'I have to go back, don't I?' she asked quietly. 'It's okay, Carly, honest. I don't mind as long as I have you to visit me . . .'

'Stacy, honey, listen to me. Lawrence—Lawrence said that you could come and stay with me. You don't have to go back.'

Frozen silence hovered between them as Stacy absorbed the words.

'Not ever?' she questioned finally, afraid to accept just yet.

'Not ever,' Caroline echoed, watching as Stacy swallowed on her fear and disbelief, the dawning wonder in her eyes making any sacrifice worthwhile.

'C-Carly . . .' she begged desperately, tears running down her cheeks, '. . . are you pos'tive?'

'Absolutely. Isn't it great?' she asked, forcing lightness into the painful moment.

'It's—terrific!' Stacy yelled, throwing her arms around Caroline's neck like an affectionate monkey, almost strangling her in her joy.

'Stacy!' Caroline protested happily. 'I can't breathe!'

'Oh, I'm sorry, Carly,' Stacy drew away, an embarrassed laugh trembling on her lips. 'Only I'm so happy. Just think, you and me can live together all alone now, without Lawrence——'

Caroline tensed, lifting a gentle hand to wipe the tears from Stacy's cheeks. 'Not—all alone, Stacy,' she corrected huskily.

Quick fear leapt in Stacy's eyes.

'What do you mean—not all alone?' she demanded suspiciously.

'I'm going to—to get married, Stacy,' Caroline explained carefully, trying to inject a happy note in her trembling voice.

'Married?' Stacy drew a shocked breath.

'Yes,' Caroline confirmed. 'To a very nice man named Barrett.'

Stacy pulled herself from Caroline's restraining arms, turning her back to walk a few paces away. 'Then I s'pose you won't want me to live with you,' she muttered sullenly, 'getting in your way . . .'

'Stacy! Of course we want you! It was Barrett who persuaded Lawrence to let us have you.'

Stacy remained silent, a distant look in her eyes, a perceptible tension stiffening her small body.

'I—I brought Barrett with me,' Caroline said nervously. 'I want you to meet him, honey. He's in the house——'

'He's right here,' a deep voice corrected softly. Barrett's hands reached to curve over Caroline's shoulders, massaging lightly as they registered the tension there.

Stacy turned to face them, her blue eyes darkening as she watched her sister face the tall man, her eyes locking with his in a desperate plea for help.

Barrett read the plea, and answered silently with a slow, reassuring smile, before turning them both to face Stacy.

'Introduce us, Caroline,' he instructed softly, his eyes steady on Stacy's tense face.

'Stacy, this is Barrett Rossiter. He's the man I'm going to—marry.'

'Hello, Stacy,' Barrett said easily.

' 'lo,' Stacy responded with curt indifference, her eyes not meeting his.

One dark eyebrow kicked up over Barrett's grey eyes.

'Caroline, why don't you go help Betty with the coffee?' he suggested calmly.

'Oh, but——' Caroline began to protest.

Barrett turned her gently towards the house. 'Go,' he told her steadily.

With a helpless shrug, Caroline obeyed.

Barrett witnessed the abortive, instinctive move Stacy made to follow, and stepped smoothly into her path to prevent it.

Stacy stared up at Barrett with sullen, angry blue eyes, measuring him with the quiet intensity only a child can produce. He calmly bore her scrutiny, appraising her in his turn.

She looked nothing like Caroline, he decided, his eyes moving over her tawny brown hair and pert little features. He had not expected her to. The difference in their appearances—Caroline, so closely resembling her father, Stacy, luckily favouring her mother—was the only thing that had saved Stacy from the abuse Caroline suffered. Stacy was too small for her age, a skinny little tomboy in torn jeans and a dirty blue T-shirt. The word 'Angel' which was scrawled across the shirt had almost been obliterated by layers of mud and repeated laundering. Significant? Barrett wondered wryly.

Stacy spoke first, her eyes wary in a way far beyond her seven years. 'Carly says you're going to take care of us now.' The statement was flat, uninterested.

'Carly?' Barrett questioned quietly, moved by the wariness in her eyes and the tenseness of her wiry body.

'Caroline, then,' Stacy amended impatiently. 'I call her that on account of I couldn't say her name properly when I was little.' Here she drew herself up to her full height, expecting a condescending remark from the huge man before her.

'I see,' Barrett replied, with just the right degree of calm interest.

'But it's only for family to use,' Stacy warned him, testing the boundaries.

'I'm going to be family when I marry Caroline,' Barrett pointed out.

'Why?' Stacy demanded bluntly, abandoning the subject of the name for the real crux of the conversation. 'Why are you going to marry Carly?'

'Because she needs me, Stacy,' Barrett answered. 'And I need her.'

'What about me?' Stacy demanded belligerently, squaring her shoulders for a fight. 'Lawrence told me once that when Carly was married she wouldn't want me any more—that *you* wouldn't want me ...' a threading fear weaved through her words.

A violent surge of anger gripped Barrett as the

frightened child spoke. If Lawrence Redden had been present at that moment, Barrett would have cheerfully strangled every malicious word from his body.

Unmindful of the dirty ground, Barrett dropped to his knees, and placed his hands on Stacy's bony shoulders, tilting her face to his. Her eyes met his defiantly, but Barrett saw the vulnerability and fear that Stacy couldn't hide.

'Then he was wrong, wasn't he?' Barrett told her calmly. 'You're more important to Caroline than anything else in the world, and more than anything she wants you to come and live with us. And so do I,' he added deliberately.

'Why?' Stacy threw the word out bravely, afraid to trust in the happiness that was within her reach finally after so much unhappy time with Lawrence.

'Oh, because Caroline loves you and I've always wanted a sister with maple syrup hair and scars on her knees and——' Barrett looked at her mock sternly, laughter in his beautiful grey eyes '—a frog in her pocket.'

A gurgle of mirthful giggles broke from Stacy as she pulled the tiny toad from her pocket and placed him on the ground, urging him along with her toe.

'I found him here, before you——' she stopped suddenly, the smile wiped from her lips as she remembered that she was supposed to be wary with this man.

'Don't stop smiling, Stacy,' Barrett asked gently. 'I like it.'

'I——' Stacy stopped, then asked in a muffled, fearful tone, 'Do you really want a sister like me, Barrett? Will I really do?'

'Oh, Stacy!' Barrett murmured softly, hurt by the words that seemed to expect a denial. 'Exactly like you.' One long finger touched her pale cheek tenderly.

'I'll be your sister, Barrett,' Stacy told him gravely, 'if you'll be my brother. Bargain?'

'Bargain,' he echoed in promise.

Stacy lifted grubby palms to her mouth, spitting into first one, then the other expertly. She rubbed her hands together ceremoniously, then held them towards Barrett.

An expression of utter seriousness on his face, Barret lifted his own hands to his mouth, spat into them with unforgotten skill, rubbed them together, and held them out to Stacy. With great solemnity, their palms met and moved together, completing the ritual.

'It's a bargain sealed,' Barrett announced.

Stacy smiled tentatively into his eyes, for the first time not afraid of what the future held.

Caroline, witnessing the exchange from her vantage point at the kitchen window, drew a deep breath and closed her eyes on a heartfelt sigh of relief.

CHAPTER SEVEN

CAROLINE's wedding day passed in a dreamlike blur. Certain incidents stood out with blinding clarity—Stacy's excited shining face, the silver triumph in Barrett's eyes as he slipped the wedding ring on to her finger in the judge's chambers where he had arranged for their marriage to take place, the gentle, concerned gleam in Betty Clark's eyes as she insisted on keeping Stacy while Barrett and Caroline spent a few days alone on their 'honeymoon'. All else faded into a dulling, blessedly enshrouding mist.

After what had seemed like hours of travelling, no word spoken between them, they had reached this cabin, nestled in the front range of the Rockies and isolated from the rest of the world by snow and the mountainous walls of its neighbours. They were truly alone for the first time, and Caroline's welcomed numbness was wearing off quickly. She was terrified.

It was wrong, terribly wrong, of Barrett to bring her to this place that cried out for tenderness and warmth. The only thing that had brought them here together was Caroline's unrequited love, and Barrett's unsatisfied desire. Soon both would be tested to their limits.

They settled in quickly, Caroline nervously ignoring the sensuous, intimate touches that turned the cabin into an erotic cage—the huge old bed that graced the one bedroom, the white bearskin rug on the floor in front of the brick fireplace.

They ate dinner in strained silence, and Caroline insisted on washing the dishes while Barrett set the fire . . .

Barrett tossed a log carelessly on to the pile already waiting in the grate before striking a match and igniting the wood. Moments later, the fire blazed crazily, casting its warming embrace to the room.

Caroline reluctantly surrendered the safety of the kitchen. A glass of wine clutched in either hand, she negotiated the tiny hallway and crossed into the low beamed living room on silent, bare feet. Barrett was crouched in front of the fireplace, the leaping orange flames from the logs reflecting in the sombre opaqueness of his eyes as he stared broodingly at the pagan dance they performed. There was something ineffably sad etched in his face, Caroline thought. Lost, maybe. She wanted to draw him into her arms, hold him close, promise him her love, give him . . . She shook herself severely. It's a trick of the firelight, she took herself to task mentally. There's nothing lost about Barrett Rossiter. He was a hard, strong man who knew exactly what he wanted and how to get it. For now, he had decided that he wanted her, and he had taken her. She would be his until he tired of the novelty of her determined resistance, and then he would be free. Caroline realised that she was only lying to herself in trying to pretend that she had seen behind the mask. There was no mask—the man was the man.

'The—the dishes are washed,' she spoke nervously, her arms crossed in unconscious defence over her chest.

Barrett tore his eyes from the flames and turned at the sound of her voice. 'You didn't have to do them,' he repeated his earlier statement, his eyes moving over her tense face.

Caroline shrugged carelessly. 'I would have had to do them tomorrow if I'd left them tonight.'

'I would have helped . . .'

'You built the fire,' she dismissed, forcing her stiff body to cross to its warmth. 'I love fires in the winter, when there's snow on the ground,' she murmured mistily, her eyes drawn to the fascinating depths of the fire's glow. 'There's such a feeling of protection . . .'

'Protection from what, Caroline?' Barrett asked, his eyes capturing hers and holding them with proving intentness. Not from me, Caroline seemed to read there. Nothing will ever protect you from me. Your love makes you an easy target.

'I——' She tore her eyes away, a hot flush engulfing her tense body. But the heat was from Barrett's eyes, not from the flames in the fireplace. Grey was not only the colour of ashes, she discovered dizzily, it was a warning of white-hot coals. 'I brought us some wine,' she said distractingly, moving to the table by the doorway where she had set the brimming glasses, and casting one longing glance into the dark freedom of the night through the window over the table before schooling her features into a smooth nonchalance and turning back to Barrett.

Crossing the room to his side, she offered him the glass. Barrett rose slowly to his feet, towering over her. Taking the glass from her nerveless fingers, he walked to the low couch and took a seat in the middle of its long length.

'Come and sit down, Caroline,' he ordered softly.

She gnawed her bottom lip torturously as she considered the suggestion. There was nothing remotely threatening in the words themselves, nor in the tone in which they had been spoken, but suddenly the tension in the room thickened perceptibly.

'The sky looks ominous,' she offered inanely. 'Do you suppose we'll get some snow?'

'Probably,' Barrett answered lazily, his eyes wry. 'Caroline, come and sit down.'

'I—I hope Betty doesn't have any trouble with Stacy. She was so excited at the wed——' Caroline broke off hurriedly, cursing herself for introducing the subject of their marriage. It was something she most definitely did not want to talk about at this particular moment.

'Betty will have no problem with Stacy. She's used to controlling high-spirited little girls, remember?' As he spoke, Barrett rose from the couch, casually set his drink on the table in front of him, and crossed to Caroline. He gently pried the glass from her tight fingers and placed it next to his own.

His hands rose to cup her face, fingers threading through her silky hair. 'What are you afraid of?'

The soft words frightened her almost as much as the darkening desire clearly shadowing his eyes.

'I—I——' she licked her lips nervously, unable to answer.

Barrett's narrowed eyes focused disturbingly on the betraying action. 'You should know better, Caroline ...' he groaned huskily, bending his head, delicately tracing the outline of her trembling lips.

Caroline breathed unsteadily, unnerved by the wild clamour of emotion he was arousing with the stroking deliberation of his mouth.

'Caroline, I am not going to hurt you,' he told her clearly, lifting his head to hold her eyes.

The soothing words, the gentle finger at the corner of her mouth, moved her deeply. What was the point in fighting? she asked herself defeatedly. She was only hurting herself, denying her own emotions. Somehow, somehow tonight she would learn to take only as much as Barrett could give, and give only as much as he wanted to take. He would never have to know that she loved him, an insidious little voice whispered temptingly.

Barrett was completely still, knowing the decision had to be hers. The tentative touch of cool fingers came as his answer. Caroline traced lightly along his hard jaw, delighting in the freedom to touch warm skin and hard bone. Her fingers moved seekingly to his long mouth, gently probing its warmth. Her eyes followed the motion hypnotically, watching as the tip of Barrett's tongue tenderly caressed the exploring fingers. Jade eyes darkened in need, tearing away to meet the leashed hunger glaring greyly from his eyes.

A silent surrender flashed between them, a joyous acceptance, a negation of the need for terms of laying down arms. The surrender was unconditional on both sides.

Caroline's hands held his face as she slowly touched her lips to his. Barrett's arms stole around her with cautious strength, moulding her willing body to his straining length. Their lips played wth each other, meeting, melding, then hiding as they moved to explore other areas. Barrett's mouth trekked hungrily from Caroline's to the rounded jaw, and then up to rain across exotic cheekbones, before slipping over to close fever-bright eyes with the sweet passion of his kiss.

Her fingers flexed against the strong male chest, a kitten with delicately sheathed claws, as his mouth explored every hollow, every curve of her face and neck.

Her own lips wandered hotly across his neck, and down to the hair-roughened breadth of his chest. Fingers deftly slipped buttons free and pushed the material of his shirt aside to allow free access to the warmth beneath.

Quickly releasing the zipper at the back of her dress, he pushed the fabric from her shoulders, following its downward path with arousing fingertips, a double caress. His hands spread gently over her ribcage, his palms delicately cupping the weight of her creamy breasts. His thumbs lifted to explore the hardened tips through the lace of her bra, and his dark head lowered slowly, dusting sweet, hot kisses over the naked swell of her breast until the fabric of her bra interfered. Such intrusion was not to be tolerated. Their fingers met over the back clasp of her bra and Barrett felt her lips curve into a smile against his chest. Her hands dropped, returning to explore the rigid strength of his shoulders and back, leaving him to complete the action of removing the scrap of material shielding her breasts. As it fell away, Barrett issued a soft groan of triumph, taking one nipple into his mouth, his tongue circling it erotically, sending sharp splinters of desire through Caroline's taut body.

'Barrett ...' she breathed dazedly, her hands clenched in helpless ecstasy on the muscled arc of his buttocks.

His darkened eyes raised to read the wild desire masking her face, satisfaction in their depths, before his mouth lowered to claim the other nipple.

Caroline's hands unclenched slowly, sliding around his waist to the buckle of his belt, releasing it with more speed than skill, and a hard shudder racked Barrett's body as her fingers moved longingly against him. He raised his head, his narrowed eyes meeting her intently, then strong fingers lifted to brush her fiery hair away from her damp forehead. Her eyes locked with his, begging silently that he free her from the silken bonds of this gnawing hunger.

A muffled groan torn from deep in Barrett's throat was her only answer. Sweeping her high in his arms, he carried her to their waiting bed, a victor savouring the sweetness of his spoils.

Laying her softly in the middle of the huge bed, he paused only long enough to strip off his one remaining article of clothing.

Caroline watched through half-closed eyes, the gleam of the fireplace bathing their bodies in its warm glow through the open door. The bed shifted as Barrett joined her, his mouth capturing hers in a silent, hot necessity, as his hands slipped her panties down her thighs, disposing of them with a careless toss across the room.

'I want you, Barrett. I want you to love me now . . .' her words escaped in ardent pleading.

'I'll love you, sweetheart,' he promised. 'I'll love you until nothing else matters, until we're both wild with the wonder of it . . .'

He moved to complete the final embrace, holding his shuddering body over hers, and Caroline's legs shifted in instinctive invitation, welcoming his thrusting rapture.

'I've got to, Caro! I can't wait any more . . .' His voice was harsh with a hunger that would no longer be suppressed.

He came to her with the first slow, passionate stroke of possession, intent on lifting her to the endless eternity of heaven.

Caroline's warm, receptive body stiffened in flashing

pain as the barriers of her innocence were breached for the first time. A small cry trembled past her lips, drawing Barrett's shocked eyes to her face. His whole body stiffened and stilled.

'Caroline ... my God, Caro!' he whispered tautly. 'I didn't know ... I never thought ... You're a virgin——'

Her long fingers lifted to his mouth, cutting off his shocked exclamation. 'No, Barrett,' she denied longingly as the initial discomfort faded and the trembling tide of hunger roared through her, and she began to move restlessly beneath his still, heavy body. 'I'm your wife,' she whispered, smiling as she felt the caressing touch of his lips against her fingers. 'Make me a woman.'

Barrett's eyes closed tightly. 'I don't want to hurt you ...' he rejected agonisedly.

'The pain's gone. Show me the pleasure ...' Her lips moved fervently over the taut planes of his face, her tongue peeping out to taste the salty dampness of his flesh.

Barrett's eye opened, flaming. 'My wife ... I'll make you my woman!' His thrusting body resumed the timeless strokes of possession, gentle at first, then wild and frenzied, that took them to the brink of the world, and beyond ...

Barrett lay awake during the silent hours before the dawn, staring sightlessly up at the ceiling as Caroline lay sleeping in his arms. Her soft cloud of red-gold hair tickled at his chin as he supported her slight weight fully against his chest. The silken smoothness of her skin tantalised his senses, the warm essence of her branded itself in his mind during the long night hours he was afraid to waste in sleep. In the darkness of the night, with Caroline trapped willingly in his arms, he was content.

But as the frail, faint fingers of dawn began to steal into the room, he tensed, watching helplessly as the pale light grew stronger, brighter. His eyes became red-rimmed and bruised as the hours passed, and his arms tightened unconsciously around Caroline's slumbering form. But Barrett could not deny the morning.

They stayed at the cabin for a week. During the day they tramped through the snow without speaking, or sat in front of the fire, exchanging stories and opinions as they listened to the strains of soft music playing in the background. A brittle tension shivered between them, acting as a protective wall that defied assault. Caroline was no closer to touching the man beneath the façade, and she in turn was wary, protecting herself from his probing eyes.

The barriers were lowered only during the hours they spent in each other's arms, plunging the depths of their desires. Caroline learned about her own needs from Barrett's patient, knowing hands, and used the knowledge he instilled to satisfy him in turn. In bed they were two finely meshed cogs, anticipating each other's needs before their own. She learned to arouse him with a look, a smile, a single touch, and revelled in her power.

But always, even in their most intimate moments, a heavy tension hovered, undeniable, unbreachable, between them.

It was their last night at the cabin. Barrett slipped outside after dinner, telling Caroline that he wanted to take a walk before retiring. The word 'alone' hung implicitly on the air between them. She watched him disappear into the night with disturbed eyes. Was the chasm between them yawning wider already? Sighing, she finished drying the dishes, and wandered into the bathroom to draw a hot bath. Perhaps its steamy embrace would ease the troubled thoughts whirling in her mind.

She luxuriated in the bath, the heat of the water draining all strength from her relaxed body. Finally she climbed out languidly, drying herself perfunctorily. The fire burning in the grate should not go to waste, she decided sleepily. She padded into the living-room and dropped to the soft fur rug before the fireplace, her naked body reflecting the glazed flames as they danced over the wood. She lay peacefully on her back, eyes closed, her arms stretched above her head in an attitude of total relaxation. The warmth of the fire seeped into her skin, flushing it a gentle rose. She stretched sinuously against the caressing fur.

Suddenly, cold, gentle hands tickled at the soles of her feet, and she yelped, startled. She had not heard Barrett's return.

'Don't move,' he commanded, restraining her stirring limbs easily. 'I'm so cold, and you are so—warm.' His hands glided up the smooth length of her calves and up, to her softly curved thighs with worshipful avidity.

Caroline subsided willingly, her entire being focused on the arousing movements of his fingers and trailing lips as they echoed the path his fingers took. From the soles of her feet to the curve of her waist they seared a possessing track, then moved higher to nuzzle at the creamy swell of her breasts. Finally, his mouth lifted to hover eagerly over her own, where a soft, mischievous smile played.

'Caro,' he murmured huskily, his eyes devouring the sweet passion in her face.

'Mmm,' she breathed, her eyes still shut. 'Who is it?' she asked innocently, her arms lifting to encircle his neck and draw him to her.

Barrett smiled in wicked enjoyment. 'Guess . . .' he invited deeply, his mouth caressing hers with a deliberate sensuality that had her writhing beneath him.

'Barrett . . .'

'Right,' he answered on a raggedly drawn breath. 'You win——'

Barrett's muffled words were the last coherent speech between them for a long, long time.

Afterwards, they lay together on the floor in the fire's glow, bodies entwined.

Caroline, feeling the even rise and fall of Barrett's chest beneath her cheek, knew he was asleep. The warmth of his body enveloped her senses completely as she let her mind drift.

Finally, she understood the exquisite agony of lovemaking without love. Would her love for Barrett and his lust for her body be enough to hold them together? Could she love them enough for both of them? Was the hell of living without his love preferable to that of living without him?

Out of all the questions that raged through her mind, this was the one whose answer Caroline knew. Yes! She could learn, with time, to accept that he did not love her, would never love her. But she could not live without him. He wanted her—he had proved that over and over again. It would be enough. She would make it enough.

Slow, silent tears leaked from her eyes, trailing down her face to land with sad little splashes on Barrett's chest.

Barrett was not asleep. He had been lying still, staring blankly at the ceiling as he absorbed the heady sensation of Caroline's soft body resting in his arms.

Their lovemaking had been perfect, a sweet, savage passion flaming wildly between them. God, he loved the feel of her, the taste, the touch of her. He ached to make her his again, ached from the soles of his feet to the tips of his fingers to be one with her, to incite the hungry kitten sounds torn from her throat as he moved inside her.

His hand lifted to sweep over her warm body when he felt the first soft splash of her tears against his skin. It dropped back to his side as they continued, his eyes closed in silent denial.

When Caroline awoke in the morning, she was alone. Vague sleep-dulled memories of Barrett carrying her to bed played at the edges of her mind. Where was he? she wondered curiously. In the past week she had grown accustomed to waking up in his arms, and she missed the warm excitement of him. Pulling on a robe, she left the room, padding on bare feet to the kitchen to make coffee.

The sight that met her eyes as she pushed open the kitchen door halted her in her tracks. Barrett sat at the table, a cup clutched between his hands. His face was grey with exhaustion, as though he had not slept at all. His eyes stared bleakly at the dark liquid at the bottom of his cup, his brow furrowed. He did not hear Caroline's entrance.

'Good m-morning,' she murmured hesitantly from the doorway, drawing his grim eyes to her face.

Obviously *not* a good morning, she deduced silently. Crossing to his side, she gathered her courage and bent to press a soft kiss against his cheek.

Barrett flinched from her touch and she withdrew immediately, humiliated.

'Wifely,' he sneered. 'How long did it take you to work up the courage to touch me?'

'You looked so—grim,' she excused herself nervously.

She was completely taken aback by the harsh laugh torn from his throat. She had floated into consciousness with a euphoric happiness, still occupied with the beauty of their lovemaking. She had thought Barrett would feel the same way, that they could build on their physical relationship a lasting commitment. She had to try.

'Barrett,' she began nervously, licking dry lips. 'Last night——'

He did not even turn to meet her eyes as he uttered the words that drew blood. 'Last night will never happen again.' The statement was flat, unapproachable.

Caroline paled.

'I—I don't understand,' she managed blankly. 'Did I do something—wrong?'

'Wrong?' Again that mirthless laugh sounded, and

she flinched from the implicit violence of it. 'Wrong? No, Caroline, you did nothing wrong. You're a very-fast learner.'

'Well, then . . .'

'Just leave it, Caroline,' he advised tautly. 'There's nothing more to be said.'

But Caroline could not leave it, could not give up without a fight. She had lost so much in her life; she could not lose Barrett. Not now.

'Is it—is it because you're—tired of me?'

Silence answered the stammered question. Uncompromising silence.

'Barrett——?'

'Yes, Caroline,' Barrett finally answered, the words falling cruelly from his weary mouth. 'If it helps at all, I'm tired of you.'

'I see,' she muttered defeatedly, tears welling in her jade eyes. 'I'll go pack.' She turned quickly to the door, running for shelter before Barrett saw her break down completely.

'Caroline!' Barrett barked, halting her in the doorway.

She did not turn. 'Yes, Barrett?'

'This doesn't change the rest of our bargain. You're still my wife; I'm still your husband. There will be no divorce.'

Caroline said nothing, her hands twisting whitely with the control she was exerting.

'You can't leave me with Redden on the loose, anyway,' he persisted. 'You wouldn't be safe. Stacy wouldn't be safe.'

'Barrett——'

'There will be no divorce,' he repeated stonily.

'No, Barrett,' she agreed dully, a silent, relieved sigh escaping her. She would still be with him. Last night she had been prepared to accept that, she reminded herself forcefully. Nothing had changed.

'Go,' he ordered tiredly.

Caroline went.

The days passed, slipping into weeks as they arranged themselves into a pattern. Caroline woke early each morning in her empty bed, vague nightmares clinging like cobwebs in the corners of her mind. As she lay, listening to the singing birds outside her window, she forced herself to concentrate on the day ahead, trying to block out the sound of Barrett's movements as he prepared for work.

He had kept his promise, had not touched her in any way since the last night of their honeymoon. If Caroline's eyes followed him hungrily, if her hands sometimes shook at any accidental contact with him, he appeared not to notice, his grey eyes coldly blank.

They had accomplished the two-hour drive from the cabin in virtual silence, stiffly polite comments only rarely breaking through the wall between them. After stopping briefly to pick Stacy up, Barrett had driven them to his house, where they would now all live. It was a comfortable, family home, outside the frantic pace of city reaches. The back yard was huge, with lots of trees perfect for climbing, Stacy informed them joyfully. The house itself was made of mellow stone and wood, a sprawling structure with five bedrooms, a family room, a formal dining-room, and an informal breakfast nook. The basement, Barrett showed them, had been converted into a recreation area. Stacy was loud with her approval. Caroline smiled politely and avoided Barrett's eyes determinedly. Their separate lives were established that first night when Barrett showed Caroline to her bedroom and disappeared into his own. The relationship was sealed in cement within a week.

Each night he came home from work exhausted. He seemed to be pushing himself relentlessly, and on the one occasion Caroline had commented on it, he had turned on her, icily polite, and informed her that she was no longer a part of his office staff, and therefore had no right to question his professional life. He had found a highly efficient woman in her early fifties to replace her, and she had been shut out totally from the business side of his life.

He ate dinner with them, always very careful in front of Stacy to portray the loving, attentive husband. Caroline never quite became accustomed to the change that swept over his hard features in Stacy's presence. His cold grey eyes grew warm and loving, his taut mouth softening indulgently. That he had come to love Stacy, Caroline had no doubts, and she was fiercely glad for that love. Stacy needed the steady guidance of a father figure, and Barrett handled her with a perfect balance of love and firmness.

Yet deep inside, Caroline could not deny the pain that sliced through her as he turned those loving eyes on Stacy. She wasn't jealous of her little sister, she told herself quickly. But she yearned to see the love in his eyes directed at her. For Stacy's sake he pretended, planting an empty kiss on Caroline's cheek as he escaped from the dining-room each night to closet himself in his study.

Caroline was dying by degrees. By the time a month had passed, she had quietly let go of any hidden dreams of winning Barrett's love. Only Stacy kept them together now, and Caroline did not know how long she could keep up the masquerade.

Caroline sunk a little deeper in the warm water of the tub. Delicately scented bubbles tickled at her chin as they floated thickly on the surface. She had been lying there, unmoving, for close to half an hour. The long soak was just what she needed to unwind before going to bed, she realised contentedly. The water seemed to be drawing the tension from her body.

Barrett was not home yet. The time he spent at the office seemed to be stretching longer and longer every day. Were it not for the fact that Caroline had met Louise Janson for herself, she would have begun to suspect that she was a shapely blonde of twenty-five, instead of a plump grandmother of fifty-two. But there was no indication that Barrett was seeking comfort with another woman. This Caroline held to her heart like a talisman. Pray God she would never have to suffer that humiliation.

At first, the vague signs of the approaching storm didn't register in her mind. The heavy silence from outside as all the night creatures streaked for shelter, the fitful flashes of lightning tearing through the dark fabric of the night and finding their way through the skylight in the ceiling of the bathroom did not penetrate her drowsy senses.

It was the ominous roar of thunder, seemingly directly overhead, that finally pulled her from her drifting. Her eyes glued to the skylight, she watched in fascination as the storm's fury was unleashed. Jagged coils of lightning seared the dark peace of the sky, searching for a partner in their frenzied dance. Thunder erupted in wild bursts, rattling windows, seeming to shake the very earth with its force. The wind joined in, gusting strong waves tearing tender young plants from their roots and tossing them carelessly aside, ripping limbs from trees and carrying them along in its violent embrace.

Caroline was mesmerised by the show of dominant force of the first storm of the spring, unable to lift herself from the rapidly cooling water she lay in.

A flaming streak of lightning lit the sky, followed almost immediately by the deafening roll of thunder. As the violence of the storm erupted into the room, it brought with it Barrett.

Caroline's gasp of surprise at the sight of him was smothered by the whipping wind as she registered his appearance. Covered only by a towel wrapped loosely around his hips, barefoot and bare-chested, he crossed half the width of the room before he noticed Caroline soaking in the huge bathtub. He stopped abruptly, his silvery eyes wary. Tension thickened as he studied the silky hair piled loosely atop Caroline's head, her shining clean face, and the delicate glow of softly rounded shoulders above the screening bubbles. Something flared wildly in Barrett's eyes.

'I—didn't know you were in here,' he spoke finally, his words muffled. 'You shouldn't be in the bath with this storm raging around us.'

'It wasn't storming when I got in the bath,' she explained awkwardly, not knowing what to say or where to look. 'I didn't know you were home,' she blurted.

'I just got in a couple of minutes ago,' he explained, his eyes fixed determinedly on her face. 'I was soaked. I thought I'd have a shower.'

'You said it was dangerous,' she reminded him breathlessly.

'Maybe I feel like living dangerously.'

'Maybe I do, too,' Caroline retorted valiantly.

'You're living dangerously now, Caroline,' Barrett told her deeply, his eyes shifting to the beginning swell of her breasts, no longer hidden from view as the bubbles began to dissolve.

He moved forward slowly, almost reluctantly, as though pushed from behind by some invisible hand, his eyes drawn unwillingly to the sight of her soft, slick body rising above the water. When he reached the side of the tub, he dropped to his knees.

'Barrett——' Caroline began huskily, not knowing what she was going to say, whether she was going to beg him to leave or ask him to stay.

His hand dipped over the side of the tub to scoop up a thin film of rapidly diminishing bubbles. 'Your bubbles are disappearing,' he said thickly, his eyes moving hotly over her body until they clashed and locked with hers. The unwavering desire that formed there melted all thoughts of denial in her mind.

'I've—I've been in here a long time,' she managed finally, then flinched as another blinding flash of lightning split the darkness of the night, to be immediately followed by a soft 'pop' as the room was plunged into darkness.

'B-Barrett?' she whispered shakily, her hands instinctively going out to clutch at his bare shoulders.

'It's all right, Caroline,' he soothed, his voice strained. 'The lightning must have hit a transformer.'

'The lights——'

'Will probably be out for a while. We'll have to break out some candles.'

'Do-do we have any?' she asked inanely.

Barrett laughed muffledly. 'Of course we have some. Stacy just had a birthday, remember?'

Caroline chuckled, thinking of the eight tiny candles they had stuck into the birthday cake. 'They ought to last us all night,' she agreed solemnly.

Her words were punctuated by another jagged flash of lightning.

'You have to get out of that water, sweetheart,' Barrett told her sternly. 'The storm is getting worse.'

'I can't!' she breathed. 'I—you——'

'Oh, Caroline,' he mocked lightly, 'it's so dark in here I can't even see the tip of my nose!' Rising to his feet, he grabbed a huge towel from the rack and spread it open invitingly. 'Come on,' he ordered briskly.

The water was quite cool now, and Caroline was more than ready to get out. Soothed by the darkness of the room and Barrett's impersonal tone, she rose slowly from the water, her body gleaming sleekly as the wetness clung to her skin. She stepped directly from the tub into the waiting towel.

Barrett's arms closed around her as he wrapped the material around her body twice before tucking the dangling edges in at the front. Caroline shuddered involuntarily as she felt the first warm brush of his hand on her breast.

The contact had been accidental, unavoidable even, she knew, but that did not stop her trembling reaction.

Barrett froze, his whole body tensing. Then, softly, carefully, his hand moved again. This time it was no accident as his fingers feathered caressingly across the swell of her breast. Caroline's eyes closed as she absorbed the sensation, so long denied, a tiny gasping moan escaping her lips as his strong fingers probed delicately at one hardening nipple.

He studied her face intently, reading the exquisite pleasure etched there. Slowly, deliberately, his hand moved to the tuck of the towel, giving her ample time to stop the movement. When she did not, he slipped the towel from her body, dropping it noiselessly to the carpet.

'Caro . . .' Barrett whispered, his tone strangled. 'Are you sure——?' His question was cut off abruptly as he felt her hands on the towel at his waist. It, too, slid to the floor unimpeded.

'Oh Caro!' he breathed huskily, as they faced each other in the darkness, naked, a raging need flaring between them more brightly than the lightning flared outside.

His hand lifted tentatively, fingers dragging across the softness of her shoulder, tracing the delicate collarbone, arousing tiny shivers as they swept up her smooth neck.

She said nothing, her only response the involuntary tightening of aroused flesh. Encouraged, his other hand rose to cup her face, holding her eyes with his. He began to explore her body with leashed hunger, moving from face to neck to shoulder, fingers running enticingly down her arms in a goosepimpling caress, to entwine with her fingers, holding her hands and guide them to his own body. Caroline needed no other encouragement. Her hands forged a path of their own over hard shoulders, down muscled back, and around to slide across his wide chest. Her fingers stopped at the flat male nipples, teasing as he had teased, wandering in ever-decreasing circles to the hard tip.

When Barrett's weight gently forced her to the luxurious carpet, she did not resist, her body eager for his possession.

'Barrett!' she pleaded on a shaking, wondering note, eyes tightly closed against the raging torrent of desire engulfing her. Then their lovemaking assumed a hot, desperate intensity as they explored the heights of rapture, their deep, ragged breathing and smothered gasps more telling than any words.

Even after the wild release, as they floated together through endless ecstasy, and slid softly replete into the silent language of fulfilment, they lay locked together, unwilling to let go of the beauty they had found.

Later, Barrett carried her into her bedroom, placing her gently on the mattress and climbing in beside her. He pulled her possessively against his warm body, moulding her softness intimately to his hard length.

No words were spoken and none were needed. Caroline lay contented against his chest, too aware of the moment to think about tomorrow or yesterday. She was in the arms of the man she loved. She cared about nothing else.

She drifted to sleep to the even thud of his heart, dreaming fancifully that each beat echoed her name . . .

It was the persistent awareness of being alone that finally pulled Caroline from the depths of slumber. Barrett was no longer beside her; she knew that without having to look.

Urgent green eyes searched the room, lightening in the pre-dawn hours. The storm had long since moved off.

Barrett sat stiffly in a hard wooden chair he had pulled to the window. The early light played cruelly upon his drawn features, emphasising the lines of weary distaste carved into his face, the taut control of his mouth.

Caroline's eyes closed on a stabbing shaft of pain as she read his grim expression. She did not speak, did not make a sound, but she knew that somehow Barrett was aware that she was awake.

'I'm sorry.' The strained harshness of his voice cut sharply across the room and destroyed the last sweet remnants of the night. He sounded—disgusted.

His eyes had not turned from their bleak contempla-

tion of the scene beyond the window. He did not look
at her, did not see the pale, stricken face, the anguished,
defeated eyes, the trembling, bruised lips.

'I didn't mean for that to happen,' he continued
emotionlessly, still not turning to face her.

'Go,' Caroline ordered roughly, knuckles white with
the control she was exerting to keep the tears at bay.

Barrett's eyes closed for one agonised minute, a
muscle kicking convulsively to life in his jaw. Slowly,
with the stiff, cautious movements of a man in torment,
he rose and crossed the room, his eyes fixed blindly on
the door. His hand closed over the knob, and he
wrenched the door open. He had taken one faltering
step from the room when he stopped and half turned.

'I know it's not enough, Caro,' he said, his tone
muffled wearily, 'but I am sorry.'

His only response was the harsh sob that broke from
her throat. Long seconds passed as he stood, listening
to the heartrending sounds. He was stiff, a man fighting
a battle within himself.

Just when Caroline thought he was going to come to
her, to hold her in his arms and comfort her, he flung
from the room, one soft expletive hanging on the air
behind him.

'Hell!'

CHAPTER EIGHT

FIDGETING nervously on the wide brown couch, Caroline flipped through a month-old issue of *Time*. She had always hated doctors' waiting rooms, and Edward Hilton's was no exception.

A sniffling child sat colouring in the corner, his mother rocking the sleeping baby in her arms. Tattered magazines littered the table tops, or were clutched in impatient hands as people read them, pretending to be interested in the months-old articles. An occasional cough or a brief murmur of conversation broke the tense silence that clogged the room. A small rotund man who sweated profusely lit a cigar and began to fill the room with its obnoxious odour, drawing annoyed glares. The scent wafted thickly around Caroline's head, and a rising wave of nausea gripped her. She leaned urgently towards the man.

'Would you please put out your cigar?' she requested with forced politeness.

The man mumbled a garbled apology and extinguished the cigar.

Caroline leaned back thankfully against the rough upholstery of the sofa, her eyes closing as the nausea subsided. She had been feeling sick for a couple of weeks now, the nausea and dizziness making her weak. She had even fainted twice, fortunately when only Stacy had been present. Caroline had sworn Stacy to secrecy, making a game of it to ensure her silence. She did not want Barrett to know.

She suspected the strain of living with Barrett was beginning to take its toll on her. She was not eating, which no doubt accounted for the awful weakness that plagued her. Her nights were restless at best, full of sleepless hours and countless nightmares.

137

Nothing had changed between Barrett and Caroline. It was as if the night of the storm had never taken place. There was a coldly polite chasm yawning between them, a discreetly veiled hostility that Caroline could not begin to breech.

For Stacy's sake they exchanged smiles over the dinner table on the rare occasions Barrett was home. If Stacy was watching, he would plant a meaningless little kiss on Caroline's cheek as he excused himself to adjourn to his study, where he remained closeted for the rest of the evening.

Weekends were spent in family pursuits, the three of them exploring the countryside, or travelling to nearby Boulder to wander along the pedestrian mall, stopping for an occasional ice cream or to watch a sidewalk mime. Caroline knew that they looked like a typical American family, and the knowledge tore at her painfully. The strain of pretending to be in love with Barrett for Stacy's sake, and pretending not to be in love with him when Stacy wasn't present, and loving him all the while she was pretending, was destroying her nerves. She was jumpy, nervous, nausea clutching her stomach in knots. She lost weight, became pale and listless.

She did not know what Barrett was thinking, did not know why he stayed with her when he was so blatantly dissatisfied with his side of their bargain, except for Stacy. She became more tense, more withdrawn in his presence, afraid her control would snap and she would beg him to love her. The fear and uncertainty were eating her up inside, and she was literally making herself sick.

'Mrs Rossiter?'

The words finally broke into her reverie, the nurse's strident, impatient tone indicating she had called Caroline's name several times before she had heard.

Rising quickly to her feet, Caroline apologised. 'I'm sorry—I was miles away.'

'Mmm,' the nurse murmured, eyeing her pale face critically. 'Follow me, please, Mrs Rossiter.'

Caroline followed the nurse through the door that separated the waiting room from the examining rooms and negotiated the narrow hallway opening on to several small examining rooms before the nurse stopped in front of a panelled door. Opening it, she motioned Caroline in.

Edward Hilton's office was dearly familiar to Caroline. She had passed through its door at various times since her childhood, as Edward nursed her through measles, mumps, growing pains and the agony of the loss of both of her parents. He was a family friend of long standing, and Caroline smiled warmly, looking down on his bent white head as he sat behind his desk, studying the papers before him. He had been a rock during the months of her mother's illness, before Lawrence had refused to let him visit again, and for that he would always have her love and gratitude.

The soft click as the nurse closed the office door behind her broke into Edward's fierce concentration. As he raised his head expectantly, his eyes collided with Caroline's. A warm welcoming smile tilted his mouth as he rose, skirting his desk to cross to her side.

'Caroline! It's good to see you,' he greeted warmly, hugging her tightly.

'Edward, it's good to see you, too. It's been too long. I haven't seen you since——' she broke off abruptly. The last time she had seen Edward had been at her mother's funeral. She had caught a misty-eyed glimpse of him as he stood, alone and away from the rest of the mourners, his eyes fixed on the wilting flowers that covered the coffin. As though feeling her gaze, Edward had glanced up and met her eyes. A silent message of sorrow and sympathy had passed between them, an infinite sadness, and Caroline's eyes had filled with tears. When her vision cleared, Edward was walking slowly away, his back stiff.

'—since your mother's funeral,' he finished heavily, pulling away to study her haunted expression. 'I'm sorry it's been so long, Caroline. But I—it's so hard for me to accept that I lost her. I keep thinking there's something I could have done, something I missed . . .'

The raw frustration in his tone touched her deeply. Lifting a hand to his shoulder, she gentled his self-directed rage.

'There was nothing you could have done, Edward. Nothing anyone could have done. You were right . . . she didn't want to live any more.'

He turned away, rubbing the back of his neck wearily. 'I know.' He appeared to be lost in a painful memory, his blue eyes inexpressibly sad. Shaking himself, he turned back to her. 'I'm sorry, Caroline. This must be painful for you. Sit down. Tell me why you've come to see me.'

Taking her elbow, he led her to one of the chairs stationed before his desk, scorning his chair behind it in favour of the one next to her.

'You're well, I hope?' he questioned. 'And happy?'

'I'm . . . fine,' she answered quietly. 'I'm married.'

Edward's brows rose. 'I didn't know. When did you marry?'

'About two months ago,' she told him apologetically. 'I'm sorry I couldn't invite you to the wedding—it was a very quiet ceremony.'

'Don't worry about it,' he advised kindly, his keen, professional eyes studying her face. 'It doesn't matter as long as you're happy.' An uncomfortable silence hung between them. 'You are happy, aren't you, Caroline?'

She licked dry lips, not knowing what to say. She couldn't lie to Edward, but she could not tell him the truth either. Barrett's and her reasons for marrying were private, and undoubtedly incomprehensible to anyone other than the two of them.

'Stacy is living with us,' she evaded carefully, her tone forcedly light. 'L-Lawrence signed over custody to me.'

Edward did not press the point. 'That's wonderful,' he congratulated her sincerely. 'How is the little terror?'

Caroline laughed at the question. 'A little terror,' she agreed affectionately. 'Always up a tree or covered with mud or hiding a frog down her shirt!' Her eyes softened. 'She loves Barrett.'

'Barrett is your husband?' he questioned with careful casualness.

'Yes,' she nodded. 'Barrett Rossiter.'

'Rossiter?' Edward's brow kicked up incredulously. 'Barrett Rossiter of the Rossiter Organisation?'

'Yes,' Caroline admitted. 'I was his secretary.'

'Romantic,' Edward commented idly.

She said nothing.

'He fell in love with you as you took dictation, dropped to his knees and begged you to marry him, huh?' Edward teased.

Caroline smiled involuntarily at the image he evoked. 'Barrett never thought of anything while he was dictating, except dictating,' she denied wryly. 'And I doubt if his knees have ever touched the ground.' Least of all at my feet, she added silently.

Edward looked disappointed. 'Then how did he propose?'

'Very calmly.'

Talking about Barrett tensed Caroline's nerves again, all ease and warmth evaporating from her body.

Edward watched silently as the smile left her lips and her eyes shadowed once again. There was something wrong, that much was clear. And that Caroline was not going to confide in him was also clear.

'Did you just come to talk, Caroline, or is there something else?'

She studied her twisting fingers.

'There's something else,' she admitted with difficulty. 'I haven't been—feeling well lately. I was hoping you could prescribe something . . .'

Edward studied her. 'What's wrong?'

'I've been feeling nauseous, dizzy,' she explained carefully, not meeting his eyes.

'Have you fainted?'

Her eyes lifted to his in surprise.

'Twice,' she confirmed. 'How did you know?'

He waved the question away. 'You look like you've lost weight. Been dieting?'

'No. I . . . I guess I haven't been too hungry lately,' she confessed.

'Mmm,' he murmured noncommittally, rising to his feet beside her. 'Come on, Caroline, let's go to an examination room—I'd like to check you over.'

'Oh no!' she protested. 'It's just tension, strain, I'm sure, Edward. Nothing to worry about. If you could just prescribe something for the nausea and dizziness——'

Edward reseated himself slowly. 'What's making you tense, Caroline?'

'Oh——' she floundered helplessly, '—just . . . things. Stacy's energy is boundless and I—haven't been sleeping well.'

He probed carefully. 'And I imagine being a new bride is stressful, especially if your husband is a busy corporate executive?'

Caroline stiffened perceptibly at the mention of Barrett. 'He's not home much,' she evaded.

'Tell me about him,' Edward invited. 'I want to know what kind of man trapped by favourite girl.'

She hesitated. What could she say? He's unbearably handsome, and I love him desperately and he can't stand to touch me?

'He's tall,' she spoke finally, 'and dark. He's very good with Stacy . . . more like a father than Law—anything else,' she substituted hastily. She was having enough trouble dodging the questions about Barrett without bringing Lawrence into the conversation.

'I'd like to meet him some time,' Edward said easily.

She swallowed thickly, imagining a bitter-sweet evening of accepting Barrett's loving act in front of Edward. 'I'd like that,' she answered faintly.

Edward's mouth tightened. 'Come on, Caroline,' he ordered, rising to his feet once more, 'let's get this examination under way.'

'Edward, it's really not necessary. I just need something to take away the nausea——'

'Caroline,' Edward's voice was kind but determined, 'you know I'm not going to prescribe anything until I've examined you, tension or not.'

She studied him exasperatedly, before giving way wryly. 'All right,' she conceded. 'Anything to preserve the peace. And get rid of this nausea!'

For twenty-five minutes Edward gently poked and prodded, insisting on running several tests. Finally he allowed her to dress.

Five minutes later, back in his office, he faced her across his desk. 'Well, I don't know what to tell you until I get the results of the tests, Caroline,' he began carefully. 'No doubt you're right and it's simply tension. I'm going to prescribe something for the nausea. It should do the trick. Let me know if there are any problems.' He quickly scribbled a prescription and handed it to her.

'Thank you, Edward,' Caroline said in relief. 'My stomach appreciates this.'

He smiled, opening the office door for her. 'Leave your new address and phone number with the nurse at the front desk and we'll get in touch with you when the test results come in,' he advised kindly.

'Oh no,' Caroline panicked. 'Couldn't I just call you?' She did not want to run the risk of Barrett discovering her visit to the doctor. He would probably take some twisted kind of pleasure in the thought that he had driven her to such extremes.

Edward's nice blue eyes became thoughtful. 'Of course. Give me a call in three or four days. I should have the results by then.'

'Thank you,' she breathed gratefully, then turned to leave.

'Caroline,' his voice called her back.

Her head tilted enquiringly as she studied the concerned look on his face. Noticing her attention, he erased it quickly. 'Don't leave it another nine months before I see you again.'

'I won't,' she promised softly, overwhelmed by a warm rush of caring for the doctor.

Smiling, she left the office.

Edward Hilton stood for one silent moment after the door closed, staring at it thoughtfully.

Finally he moved to his desk and pressed down the call button on his intercom.

'Would you come in, please, Louise?' he asked his nurse politely.

The door opened almost immediately.

'Yes, Dr Hilton?'

'I'd like the results of Mrs Rossiter's tests by tomorrow. Would you tell the lab to rush it, please?'

'Of course, Dr Hilton,' the nurse responded obediently, before turning and leaving the office.

Edward's eyes were disturbed as he stared at Caroline's chart.

When Caroline arrived home, she sat in the car for one moment, her hands curled whitely around the steering wheel. She was exhausted. The nausea and dizziness, the lack of sleep and food had taken more out of her than she had admitted even to Edward. She wanted nothing more than to bury her head in a soft pillow and cry until she ran out of tears. Then she wanted to sleep for a solid week. And the sad part of it was, she didn't feel as though she had the strength to get out of the car! A slightly hysterical laugh bubbled past her lips.

Get a hold on yourself, she ordered sternly. Barrett will have you slapped in a padded cell and then what would you do? The answer came instantly.

'I would still love him,' she groaned tiredly. She would always love him. The sooner she accepted that, the sooner she could try to find a way to live without him.

Squaring her shoulders, she pushed herself from the car and climbed the steps to the front door. Entering the hall, she headed straight for the stairs, intending to go directly to her room. For once she was grateful for Stacy's absence, having dropped her sister off at a friend's slumber party before her evening appointment with Edward.

Her foot was on the bottom step when Barrett came charging out of the living-room.

'Where the hell have you been?' The question was bitten out furiously.

Caroline turned sharply at the words, a fighting flame flickering to life inside her.

'It's none of your business,' she told him icily, her eyes taking in the open dress shirt with its rolled-back sleeves and the slightly rumpled black pants. He had obviously not changed since coming home from the office, only taking enough time to remove his jacket and tie and kick off his shoes. Shoeless, he still towered over her, his rage making him seem even taller as he moved to within inches of her to glare down balefully.

'None of my business!' he repeated angrily. 'Of course it's damn well my business. You're my wife!'

'I didn't think you'd remembered,' Caroline accused wearily.

His eyes hardened. 'What's that supposed to mean?'

'Nothing,' she refused to be drawn into such a dangerous discussion, regretting having spoken in the first place. 'What are you doing home so early?' It was seven o'clock, but lately Barrett had not left his office much before nine, and Caroline had not expected tonight to be any different.

He allowed himself to be averted from the potentially explosive discussion. 'I came home to take you and Stacy out to dinner, and I found the house empty. No notes, no explanations. And it's none of my business!' His rage began to boil again.

She had been wrong, Caroline amended silently. Barrett had also taken time to drink something when he had got home and found the house empty. She could smell the whisky on his breath.

'Surely you didn't think we had left you, Barrett,' she said mockingly, too tired, too angry to monitor her words.

Barrett's entire body went rock-taut, and for one horrible moment he said nothing at all, his eyes flaming.

'No,' he agreed finally, his tone dangerous, 'I didn't think you'd left me. We both know there's no chance of that, don't we?'

Caroline's eyes closed on a wave of nausea. What did he mean by that? she wondered sickly.

'Not as long as your dear stepdaddy is out there, running free and holding a grudge,' he spelled out derisively.

She drew a ragged breath. 'Then why are you so furious, Barrett?'

'Because I didn't know where you were. And I'm hungry!' he shouted, running a distracted hand through the already disordered smoothness of his inky hair.

'Go and have another whisky,' she advised angrily, turning to the stairs once again. 'That ought to take the edge off your appetite!'

A rough hand shot out to spin her around to face him. 'There are appetites and there are appetites,' he drawled warningly. 'I'd be careful about which ones I aroused, if I were you, Caroline.'

'Let me go, Barrett,' she enunciated tightly.

'Explain what you meant by that bitchy comment of yours.'

'Barrett . . .'

'Explain while I get myself another drink,' he added mockingly. 'I'm sure this explanation will go down better with a good whisky.'

Practically dragging her across the foyer, he hauled her ungently into the living room, leaving her to rub her arm where he had held her as he crossed to the bar and fixed another drink.

'Well?' he demanded, a brow raised in arrogant interrogation.

'Well what?' Caroline repeated sulkily. 'You were drinking before I came in.'

'Yes, I was drinking,' Barrett agreed harshly. 'You seem to have a talent for driving men to it.'

The cruel words cut into her deeply. She turned wordlessly, intent on escape, and a muffled curse was torn from Barrett as he glimpsed the ashen hurt in her face. Shoving the drink down on a nearby table, he came up behind her with two gigantic strides, his hands curling tightly around her shoulders to stop her from leaving. A violent shudder racked her body as the feel of his hands burned a vivid awareness into her skin, and he registered the tremor with narrowed eyes.

'I'm sorry, Caroline,' he apologised softly, his voice husky and contrite. 'That was a rotten thing to say. I only had one drink before you came in. I had a bad day at the office and I was ... disappointed when I found the house empty.' The explanation was delivered in a soothing tone, calming the tremors rocking her body. When the shaking subsided, he turned her gently in his arms, meeting her eyes.

'I am not Lawrence,' he stated quietly. 'I don't need to drink to escape. If you want, I'll never touch a drink again.'

Caroline flushed, embarrassed by the insight he had shown into her reasoning—or lack of reasoning, she amended wearily. Barrett was not Lawrence. He had a strength of character Lawrence had never possessed. He would never fall into the fool's trap of alcohol.

'I——' she broke off, biting her lip.

'I don't want you to be afraid of me, Caroline,' Barrett told her gently. 'You've had enough fear in your life.'

'I'm not afraid of you,' she denied honestly. She *wasn't* afraid of him. The violence in him was not brutal, it would never be turned towards her or Stacy. His release was the creative outlet of his work, she suspected. If anything, it was the emotions he had aroused in her that she feared, the overwhelming, uncontrollable need he had shown her.

'Good,' he approved, moving away to stand by the couch. But if Caroline had thought he had forgotten his original question, she was sadly mistaken. 'Where were you?' His voice was implacable.

Her body stiffened in defiance. 'I—I dropped Stacy off at a friend's house for the night—the slumber party, remember?—and then I went ... shopping,' she invented quickly.

'I'd forgotten about the slumber party,' Barrett admitted ruefully. 'What did you buy?' The question was shot at her rapidly, as though to catch her off her guard.

It succeeded. She floundered.

'I—there was nothing I wanted.'

'What an inexpensive little wife you are!' he marvelled dryly.

'I didn't marry you for your money,' she reminded him stiffly.

'Oh, I know why you married me, Caroline,' he taunted. 'You made it quite clear.'

What did he mean? she wondered frustratedly. Why did he have this terrifying habit of dropping phrases that could be interpreted so many different ways? You're just tense, she calmed herself. Hiding your love for him is making you paranoid. Calm down. He doesn't know.

'This conversation is pointless,' she told him bravely. 'I'm tired—I think I'll go to bed.'

'Not so fast, Caroline. We still have things to discuss.' Barrett warned hardly.

'Like what?' she questioned warily, shoulders slumped.

'Like where you were tonight,' he repeated in steely determination.

'Barrett ...'

'You weren't shopping,' he stated flatly.

She remained obstinately silent.

'Where, Caroline?' A pause. 'With whom?'

That jerked her back to full attention. Surely he did not know she had gone to see Edward tonight? 'What— what do you mean?' she stammered guiltily.

Barrett rounded on her angrily. 'Is that it? Have you been out with someone?'

'Who would I be out with?' she demanded, trying to reason with him in the face of his anger.

'A man,' he snarled. 'Is there someone, Caroline?' His question was ground out with deadly menace.

'No!' she denied swiftly, not liking the direction the conversation was taking. 'I—I went for a drive . . .'

'My God!' he cursed, striding to her side to grab her arms with hurtful fingers. 'I'm not that much of a fool, sweetheart. If I'd known you were missing it so much, I wouldn't have denied myself your bed!'

'Well, why did you?' she screamed, enraged. 'I never asked you to!'

The muscle in his jaw pulsed convulsively. 'Because your tears brand more painfully than any iron, Caroline. And I don't need any more scars.'

Caroline gazed at him blankly, completely mystified. What was he talking about? There wasn't a scar any where on the smooth golden length of his body, and none she had put there, God knew.

'Barrett——' she began cautiously, shifting beneath the white-hot blaze in his eyes, '—I don't think . . .'

'No, don't think, Caro,' he whispered hoarsely, his eyes fixed hungrily on her softly parted lips. 'Just feel. Feel me. Feel this——'

His dark head lowered slowly, until his lips took hers in a trembling, hungry possession that shocked waves of sensation through her entire body, ripping apart the walls that had for so long banked the physical demands of her body. Barrett's mouth played longingly with hers, caressing its fullness, while his hand lifted to possess the aching fullness of one taut breast, toying erotically with the hardening nipple, eliciting a startled gasp from Caroline as she arched instinctively closer.

A loud knock sounding on the front door broke into the smothering, heated silence. Barrett's hands stilled on her body. 'No,' he gasped, agonised. 'Not . . . now——'

'Barrett . . .' Caroline whimpered. 'Please, don't leave me!'

The knock came again, loud and determined. With a savage curse, Barrett tore himself away from the welcoming warmth of her slender, yearning body. Threading shaky fingers through his hair, he fought to regain control of his breathing. His eyes were darkly passionate as they raked ravenously over her hotly aroused body. Without a word, he turned on his heel and stalked from the room.

'This had better be good!' he roared, throwing the door open violently to confront the source of the interruption.

There was a swift, shocked silence, then the words of the visitor filtered into Caroline where she stood in the middle of the living room, shielded from sight by the door Barrett had half-closed behind him.

'Excuse me,' a masculine voice murmured politely. 'I'm looking for——' there was a slight pause and the faint rustling sound of papers being shuffled together, then, '——Caroline Forsythe Rossiter. Is she here?'

Caroline had reached the doorway to the hall on purely reflex action when Barrett's voice reached her.

'I'm Barrett Rossiter. My wife is—busy. Can I help you?'

'Well, I suppose——' the voice began reluctantly.

'I'm not busy, Barrett,' Caroline denied, moving into the middle of the hall, where Barrett's body did not block her view of their visitor.

Her breath caught painfully as she saw the uniformed State patrolman standing uncomfortably on the doorstep. A sickening premonition of dread curled in the pit of her stomach, and her face whitened alarmingly.

The patrolman studied her over Barrett's shoulder as she spoke, and Barrett turned his head, taking in the frightened glitter that had taken the place of the drugged desire in her jade eyes.

Opening the door wider, he moved out of the man's path. 'Come in,' he invited curtly, closing the door sharply behind the patrolman before crossing to

Caroline's side and placing a comforting arm around her shaking shoulders.

'What is it, officer?' Barrett spoke grimly, his mouth tight.

'There's been an accident,' the man began compassionately, his eyes on Caroline's white face.

'Is—is it . . . Stacy?' she stammered pitifully, her eyes anguished.

Barrett's arm tightened painfully around her, and she heard the strangled curse he bit off as his eyes snapped to the man's face.

'Stacy?' the patrolman repeated, perplexed. 'No, ma'am. There was no one by that name involved.'

'Thank God!' Caroline shuddered, sagging weakly against the hard length of Barrett's body, not seeing the grim, dawning perception in Barrett's eyes.

'I'm afraid it's your stepfather, Mrs Rossiter,' the patrolman continued hesitantly, clearly uncomfortable with his task. 'He was drunk, his car—wrapped around a telephone post . . .'

Caroline heard the words, even understood what they meant, but they seemed so distant, so removed. Her whole body was wrapped in ice, and she was peacefully, thankfully numb.

'Is he dead?' she asked emotionlessly, feeling it was expected of her.

'Yes, ma'am,' the officer spoke gently, relieved that she had spoken the word first. 'I'm sorry.'

'Was—was anyone else hurt?' she asked quietly.

'No, he was alone. We found your name in his papers . . .'

'Yes,' Barrett finally spoke, his voice grating harshly in comparison to Caroline's muffled questions and the other man's compassionate answers. 'Thank you for telling us.' Removing his arm from Caroline's shoulder, he crossed to the front door and opened it pointedly.

The patrolman hesitated for one second, studying Caroline, as she remained stiffly in the hall.

'I'm sorry, Mrs Rossiter.'

Caroline nodded silently, completely unable to respond to the sympathy in his voice.

Slowly he turned, leaving the house without another word.

Silence stretched unbearably after the soft closing of the door. Finally, Caroline gathered her courage and lifted her eyes to Barrett's face.

He was staring blindly at the opposite wall, his face a twisted mask of bitter agony.

She knew exactly what he was thinking. He needn't have married her, after all. If he had only waited two months, the problem would have solved itself. And it had only taken one week for his desire to burn itself out. The harsh pain carving his features was evidence of his resentment.

'I'm sorry!' she cried, tears pouring heedlessly from her eyes, as she turned and ran.

CHAPTER NINE

BARRETT silenced the strident call of the intercom with a stabbing finger.

'What is it, Mrs Janson?' he queried impatiently, his eyes running over the document in his hand.

'I know you asked not to be disturbed, Mr Rossiter ...' Louise Janson began apologetically, 'but there's someone on the line who insists that he has to speak to you—a Dr Hilton. What should I——?'

'Hilton?' Barrett repeated the name thoughtfully. 'Do I know him?'

'I don't think so, Mr Rossiter. But he does seem very anxious to speak with you ...'

'Okay, Louise, I'll take it. Thank you.' Barrett rubbed a tired hand around the back of his neck before engaging the line.

'This is Barrett Rossiter. What can I do for you?' he spoke crisply into the receiver.

'Mr Rossiter, my name is Dr Edward Hilton.' The voice on the line was that of an older man.

'Yes, Dr Hilton?'

'Mr Rossiter, if it's possible, I would like to see you. There is something I'd like to discuss with you.'

'Correct me if I'm wrong, Dr Hilton,' Barrett began politely, 'but I don't remember ever having met you. I can't think of anything we would have to discuss ...'

'I'm sorry, Mr Rossiter,' Dr Hilton excused the oversight quickly. 'I thought Caroline might have mentioned my name to you——'

'Caroline?' Barrett picked up on the name harshly. 'What does this have to do with Caro? Is there something wrong? Has she had an accident?' he demanded roughly, fear threading through his words.

'No, no, nothing like that,' Edward Hilton soothed

hurriedly. 'Your wife came in for some tests yesterday, and I've just gotten the results. I'd like to talk to you about them,' he spelled out his reasons for the call clearly.

'Tests? What kind of tests?' Barrett was grappling with the fact that Caroline had gone to a doctor without mentioning it to him.

'That's what I'd like to talk to you about,' Dr Hilton answered smoothly. 'When can you see me?'

'Where are you?' Barrett hurriedly noted the address on the pad in front of him.

'This is my half day,' Dr Hilton warned. 'The office will be empty. I'll make sure the door is open, just walk on back.'

'I'll be there in twenty minutes,' Barrett promised, folding the paper and pushing it into his jacket pocket.

'I'll be looking for you, then.'

Barrett replaced the receiver numbly. Tests . . . Caro had not told him. She must have been feeling ill to have gone to a doctor, and she had not told him. She had seemed tired lately, withdrawn, maybe. But he had attributed that to the strained relationship between them. What if it were something more? The words seared his brain. What if Caro were ill, seriously ill? Wouldn't the doctor call him in just such a way, arranging to speak with him face to face to break the news in a coldly professional way? What if she were dying?

Barrett swallowed convulsively, his hands gripping the desk desperately.

He dragged on his coat automatically as he left the office, passing Mrs Janson's desk without a word.

'Mr Rossiter?' she questioned warily, eyeing him with amazement as he reached the door.

'Oh, Mrs Janson,' he identified her distractedly as he stepped into the hallway, 'cancel all of my appointments,' he directed. 'I won't be in for the rest of the day.'

'But——' Louise Janson never finished the sentence.

The door was closed before even that short word had left her lips. She snapped her mouth shut and looked at the overflowing appointment schedule before her, reaching for the telephone with resignation. From the length of the list, it would probably take the better part of an hour to cancel them all. One hand prudently plucked the earring from her lobe as she began to dial . . .

Barrett reached Dr Hilton's office in fourteen minutes. He stood outside the office door for one frozen moment, unable to knock. His eyes closed as he tried to erase the fearful thoughts crowding his mind. He was the man who could deal with anything, he reminded himself forcefully. He would somehow deal with this.

A determined double rap sounded loudly on the office door and was answered almost immediately.

'Come in,' the voice from the telephone bid him.

Barrett pushed the panelled door inward and stepped into the office, feeling as though he were walking to a scaffold.

The room was designed as every doctor's office should be, conveying a strong sense of calm authority. An overflowing bookcase lined an entire side wall, testifying to the occupant's learned intelligence. Comfortable chairs were scattered informally, yet somehow managed to strike a note of dignity. A massive oak desk sat in the weakly streaming sunlight before the double windows, drawing the eye immediately.

Barrett moved to it slowly, his footsteps muffled by the sober brown carpet covering the floor. His guarded eyes examined the man seated behind the desk.

Edward Hilton rose as Barrett approached, meeting the measuring look with one of his own. He was a tall man, leanly built. He appeared to be in his late fifties, with an abundance of shining white hair and a pair of wire-rimmed glasses perched on his nose. His eyes were direct and incredibly blue, gleaming with a warm

professionalism, and something more that Barrett could
not immediately define. His whole demeanour spoke of
calm efficiency, and Barrett offered his hand, instinctively trusting him.

'Mr Rossiter?' Dr Hilton spoke first, receiving an
affirmative nod from Barrett. 'I'm Edward Hilton.
Please, sit down. I want to thank you for coming. I——'

'You said it was about Caro,' Barrett cut in severely,
'something about some tests . . .'

'Yes, that's right. I just received the results this
afternoon,' Edward Hilton confirmed. 'Although I must
say, I suspected yesterday when I examined her . . .
Would you like some coffee?' he offered politely,
gesturing to the coffee pot on the counter.

Barrett felt as though this man were deliberately
playing with his nerves, much like a naughty child
pulling the wings off a fly. The feeling of prolonged
torment was the same.

'No, thank you,' he rejected the coffee impatiently.
'What kind of tests?'

'Let me clarify something first,' Edward advised
slowly. 'I don't believe Caroline has mentioned me to
you, has she?'

Barrett shook his head negatively.

'No, I didn't think so,' Edward echoed thoughtfully,
his hands steepled on the desk in front of him. 'Well,
I've been Caroline's doctor since she was a child—
delivered her myself, in fact. I know that girl well, very
well. She's almost like a daughter to me——' he
stopped speaking as Barrett shifted restlessly in his
chair. 'I'm telling you this because I want you to
understand why I called you here. I normally would not
have done so. I don't think it's quite . . . ethical. Maybe
it is,' he dismissed with a smile. 'I often have trouble
deciding what is and what is not.

'However,' he continued, 'Caroline is very important
to me. I asked you here more as a friend than as a
doctor. I want you to understand that,' he reiterated
earnestly.

'I understand,' Barrett assured him irritably.

Edward's bright eyes passed over him consideringly, noting the strong lines of his face, now pinched with tension and self-control, and the smoky demand of his eyes. Finally, Edward seemed to come to a conclusion, issuing a small nod.

'I received the impression that you and Caroline are having—difficulties.'

Barrett's eyes shifted to the diplomas on the wall behind the desk, moving over them blindly. He said nothing.

'For that reason,' Dr Hilton continued deliberately, 'I don't think she would have told you that she hasn't been feeling well lately.'

Barrett's eyes snapped back to him as he listened intently to Edward's words.

'Tiredness, nausea, dizziness,' Edward enumerated her symptoms clearly. 'She's fainted twice,' he added softly, steady blue eyes watching for reaction.

Barrett stiffened. 'She didn't—tell me,' he admitted finally.

'I thought not. She came in, asked me if I could prescribe something. She didn't want to bother with an examination, seemed to think it was just exhaustion, tension. Oh, don't worry,' Dr Hilton waved Barrett to silence as he began to protest. 'I insisted on the exam, ran a few tests . . .' he paused, carefully choosing his next words. 'It wasn't exhaustion that was making her feel ill . . .'

Barrett's throat worked convulsively, his body tensing painfully in the chair.

'It's something serious, isn't it?' he demanded roughly, his eyes meeting the doctor's fiercely, daring him to deny it. 'Something you can't quite figure out how to tell me. Funny,' he threw out a bitter laugh that wasn't a laugh at all, 'I would have thought you would be good at this!'

Dr Hilton opened his mouth to speak, but Barrett persisted.

'Ah, but it's Caro this time, isn't it? You're personally involved, and you don't know how to say . . . to tell me . . .' his accusing voice, trailed off stiffly. Edward caught sight of his steely eyes, almost flinching from the raw agony glaring there.

'Mr Rossiter——' he began placatingly.

Barrett did not seem to hear as he shot to his feet, looming over the doctor threateningly. His eyes turned to Edward, darkening with hard determination.

'You are *not* going to take her from me,' he stressed savagely. 'No one, nothing can take her from me. She is mine. I made her mine two months ago and she will always be mine,' he warned hoarsely. 'So you just give me the name of a specialist who can help us, someone who isn't so ready to—to . . .' His jeering tone cracked pathetically, a muscle kicking to pulsating life in his jaw. He turned his burning eyes from Edward's face, staring helplessly at the wall, his fists clenched tightly.

'Don't take her from me.' The bleak tone barely reached Edward, muffled by distance and fear. 'Please, don't——' One tear slipped from his eye, winding a tortured trek down his face. Barrett's hand did not move to erase it. 'I won't live without her . . .'

'Please, Mr Rossiter!' Edward commanded, finally released from the paralysing tension that had held him in its grip as Barrett had begged for Caroline's life. 'Caroline is not dying! I never meant for you to think that.'

Barrett's tortured eyes raced wildly over Edward's face, analysing the honesty and compassion he saw there, not daring to believe the truth of his statement.

Edward regarded him steadily, sensing his lingering fear.

'This is not something I would lie about,' he promised calmly. 'Caroline is not dying.'

Barrett sagged against the wall, his strong, hard body weak with relief. 'Thank God,' he muttered throatily. 'Thank God!'

'This certainly answers one of the questions I wanted to ask you,' Edward murmured consideringly. 'You do love her, don't you?'

'Desperately,' Barrett confirmed shakily, slowly straightening from the wall. 'What's wrong with her, Dr Hilton? Why has she been fainting?'

'Why, because she's pregnant,' Edward answered simply, his eyes sharpening as he watched Barrett's reaction. 'And please don't collapse against that wall again,' he begged amusedly. 'I'm not sure it can stand the weight!'

Barrett did not hear. He was staring at the doctor, completely stunned.

'Pregnant?' he repeated blankly, as though he had never heard the word before. 'You mean, with a baby?'

Edward's mouth kicked up slightly at the corners. 'With a baby,' he agreed gravely.

Barrett sank back into his chair, his legs feeling as though they would no longer support him.

'Pregnant,' he echoed, staring at nothing. 'Caro is pregnant.'

'By my calculations, about seven weeks,' Edward supplied.

Seven weeks. Barrett's mind drifted back to their honeymoon in the mountains and his face softened miraculously. Memories of the cabin, the snow, the fire, Caroline's soft skin and warm, willing body flooded his mind. He was fiercely glad that they had conceived their baby then. His heart pounded painfully as he tested the words. Their baby. It sounded so . . . right.

'What did she——' he cleared his throat tensely. 'What did Caroline say when you told her?' he questioned warily.

'I haven't told her,' Edward admitted slowly. 'She had no idea when she came in that she might be pregnant. I don't think it even occurred to her . . .'

'She won't want this baby,' Barrett muttered his thoughts aloud, his eyes tormented. 'But I want it. God, how I want this baby . . .'

'Why won't she want the baby?' Edward asked quietly, bravely meeting Barrett's eyes.

The silence in the office became stark and smothering. Barrett did not answer.

'Does she love you?' Edward probed.

Barrett stiffened. 'Does it matter?' he questioned dangerously.

'Yes. Does she love you?'

A long pause.

'There are different kinds of love,' Barrett evaded, 'different degrees of loving——'

'Does she love you?' Edward persisted rigidly.

'All right, no!' Barrett snapped. 'She doesn't love me.' He ran a weary hand over his eyes. 'Are you satisfied?'

'Hardly,' Edward returned dryly. 'She married you . . .'

'I forced her to marry me,' Barrett amended tightly.

'How?'

'She needed a husband. She was fighting to get custody of her little sister,' he explained tiredly before Edward could ask.

'Ah,' Edward breathed in comprehension. 'I delivered Stacy, too.'

'You must know how much Caro loves Stacy, what she would do for her . . .'

'Even marry a man she didn't love?' Edward queried doubtfully.

'Even marry a man she didn't love,' Barrett agreed grimly.

'And become pregnant with his child? I don't think so, Mr Rossiter.'

'Yes, well,' Barrett closed his eyes briefly, 'I forced that on her, too.'

Edward stiffened, his professional calm becoming lost in a smothering anger. 'You raped her?'

'God, no!' Barrett exploded chokingly. 'I would never——'

'Well then——' Edward began, his anger dissolving.

'I—won her body, but not her mind. She fought me even as she was——' he broke off sharply. 'What's that delightful word?' Barrett pondered grimly. 'Ah, yes—seduce. I seduced my wife.'

'It's not a crime . . .' Edward's tone suggested slight mockery.

'I told her . . . I made it the condition of our marriage. Blackmail is a crime,' Barrett derided himself. 'But I wanted her so badly,' he explained shakily. 'I thought—I thought if I could just make her mine . . . show her how much I needed her . . . I thought she would stay with me . . .' he drifted off hopelessly.

'In other words, you thought you could blind an innocent girl with the expertise of your sexual prowess,' Edward restated hardly, giving him no quarter.

'All right, yes!' Barrett admitted, defeated. 'I thought it was the only way . . .'

'It seems you've discovered another way,' Edward said harshly. 'I know Caroline very well. She won't leave you now, not ever. She'll stay with you and try to make it work, no matter what she feels for you.'

'The baby . . .' Barrett whispered sickly, finally understanding the enormity of the burden he had thrust on Caroline with his selfish need for the warmth and wonder of her.

'The baby,' Edward confirmed. 'Tell me, Mr Rossiter, why was Caroline so desperate to get custody of Stacy—so desperate that she married a man she didn't love?'

Barrett flinched from the unvarnished bluntness of the doctor's question.

'She was afraid,' he muttered finally. 'Her stepfather began to drink more and more after her mother died . . .' Dr Hilton paled at his words, but Barrett did not notice, lost in Caroline's painful past. 'Caro was terrified of what he would do to Stacy if she were ever around when he went into one of his drunken rages, how seeing the only father she ever knew in that condition would scar her young mind. She had to get

Stacy away, and Redden refused to give up custody. He used to torment Caro by pretending that he would let her have Stacy, then tell her he'd changed his mind ...'

'I will never understand why Marie married that bastard!' Edward swore ferociously. 'Six months after Robert died she married Lawrence Redden. And every day after that was a living hell for her!'

'She was alone,' Barrett explained carefully, as Caroline had explained to him. He sensed the underlying savagery of Edward's words, suggesting much more than professional concern. 'She had two young children to raise, bills to pay, and no training for any kind of job. She married Redden because she had no choice.'

'And like a fool, I was waiting for a decent interval to pass, praying that she would get over Robert and be ready to love again ...' Edward castigated himself ruthlessly, the words falling bitterly from his mouth.

Barrett studied him in unsuppressed astonishment.

'Yes, I loved her,' Edward admitted resignedly, meeting his eyes briefly, then looking away. 'For years I loved her. But she was happily married to Robert Forsythe, and I was her doctor. And no matter how much trouble I may have defining what is "ethical",' he spat the word out scornfully, 'I knew that loving Marie was not. I should have refused to continue as her physician once I realised how I felt, I know. That's what all the books tell you. But I couldn't deny myself the exquisite agony of seeing her, being with her ...' His mouth twisted, deriding his own weakness. 'God, you can't imagine what it was like, watching her fade away before me, seeing the lines of pain and hopelessness carve themselves into her beautiful smooth skin, knowing there was nothing I could do to stop her from slipping away from me ...' His face was drawn and infinitely sad as he became lost in painful memories.

'Perhaps now you can understand why I called you here, why Caroline is so important to me. I used to pretend that she was *my* daughter. I don't want her to suffer the way Marie suffered.'

Barrett's face contorted. 'Why didn't you do something to protect her from Redden? Why did you sit by and allow him to abuse her the way he did——?'

Edward's body jerked tensely, his eyes cutting furiously over Barrett's accusing face. 'Abuse her?' he repeated sharply. 'What the hell are you talking about?'

'You didn't know? You really didn't know?' Barrett rasped incredulously. 'In the six months after her mother died, before I found her,' he swallowed grimly, '—Redden beat Caroline. He got drunk and he——' A violent expletive cut him short.

'Why didn't she tell me?' Edward burst out harshly. 'Dear God, why didn't she tell me? I would have stopped him, gotten her away from him somehow ...'

'She didn't tell you because of Stacy. All that she could think about was a sweet six-year-old who had just lost her mother. The last thing she needed was trouble of that kind. Redden wasn't abusing Stacy—nothing would have stopped Caro from taking Stacy and running if he had been—and she thought if she got a good job, started to earn good money, that Redden would give up custody. I don't know,' he admitted dispiritedly, his hands clenched tightly. 'How do you begin to understand the terrified reasoning of someone who went through what Caro did?'

His body was taut with the agony that stabbed at him each time he thought of Lawrence Redden and the pain he had inflicted so casually.

'My God,' Edward breathed raggedly. 'If he wasn't already dead, I would beat the hell out of him!'

'It's all right,' Barrett assured him, his mouth curling with remembered pleasure. 'I did.'

Edward studied him slowly, a grateful respect glimmering in his eyes. 'Thank you,' he said quietly.

'Don't thank me, doctor,' Barrett dismissed. 'I enjoyed it immensely.'

Neither spoke for a moment, both struggling to regain control of their anger.

'Dr Hilton,' Barrett began curiously, 'why did you call me? Why didn't you just tell Caro about the baby?'

'I had to be sure that you were the right man for Caroline, to know if you loved her the way she deserves to be loved,' Edward told him deeply.

'And?'

'I think you love her as much as I loved her mother. More, maybe,' he amended tightly, 'because you had the courage to take what she wouldn't give.'

'Thank you, Dr Hilton.' It was Barrett's turn to express his gratitude.

'Don't thank me, Mr Rossiter,' he mocked Barrett's previous words deliberately. 'I enjoyed it immensely.'

Barrett grinned back at him in total accord. Then, rising to his feet, he stretched out his right hand and shook the doctor's firmly.

'I guess I'd better get home—tell Caroline about . . . the baby.'

'One thing, Barrett,' Edward's voice halted him as he prepared to leave. 'Giving birth is not easy at the best of times. The strain of your present relationship with Caroline will not make it any easier.'

Barrett released a pent-up breath and met Edward's blue eyes squarely, his own eyes bleak.

'I meant what I said, you know,' he confided painfully. 'I won't live without her.'

'And what if she can't live with you?' Edward asked quietly, his face concerned.

For a long moment, Barrett did not speak.

'I don't know,' he answered finally in grim tones. 'I just don't know.'

Edward watched as he walked from the office, closing the door noiselessly behind him.

'I don't think you could live without her, Barrett Rossiter,' he murmured to the closed door. 'I really don't think you could.'

CHAPTER TEN

CAROLINE sat dejectedly on the window seat, legs curled tensely beneath her as she studied the wet, grey day with glum eyes. Lawrence was dead. Dead. The word rolled through her mind with the gentle inevitability of a mist in a valley. Lawrence was dead . . . destroyed by the alcohol he had for so long used as a crutch, but more, more than that, destroyed by the twisted hatred in his own mind. The hatred had been just as much of a crutch as the liquor had been, Caroline realised finally. The haunted jealousy that he had built and thrived on for so long had fed him, held him, played both scapegoat and friend, protector and enemy, and bore the weight of his own inadequacies. Lawrence had been neither strong enough to win Marie, nor loving enough to let her go. Now that she finally understood the pathetic ghosts that drove him, Caroline could release the fear and distrust he had instilled in her, and free herself from their warping influence. She had been his only available target, she realised sadly, and could almost find it in herself to be grateful to Lawrence that he had not ground out his rage on Stacy. What she could not, would not forgive was the anguish he had subjected Marie to during the six agonising years she had been married to him before she had escaped. He had taken her from her children, deliberately stamped out the flame of her life. And more damnably, he had taken her from herself, holding her soul in careless, brutal hands. For that Caroline would always hate him.

Lawrence was dead. Caroline almost felt guilty at the undeniable wave of relief that hit her as she thought of this. Never again would she have to fear for Stacy's safety, or for her own. She had studied her own wounds, drained the festering poison, and sealed them clean. She was free of the pain he had inflicted during his life.

How ironic that Lawrence should die just two short months after Barrett had sacrificed his freedom to protect Caroline and Stacy from him. Caroline had seen the graven agony of his face as he listened to the patrolman announcing Lawrence's death, and she knew that Barrett was regretting the bargain he had made with her as he realised that he was tied to a woman he did not love—and now tied for nothing!

If I were stronger, she thought dully, if I loved him less, I would leave before Barrett asked for his freedom. Lawrence would laugh if he knew that he had caught Barrett in his twisted chains, too. Or did I do that, she wondered achingly, by loving him when he didn't want to be loved?

She shuddered as the familiar cold sickness clutched her stomach. It didn't matter any more. They were caught as securely and as painfully as a wild animal in a hunter's trap, and until one of them had the strength or the will to grasp for freedom, they would remain locked together in a harsh, bitter battle with each other and with themselves. And Caroline knew that she would never be the one to wrestle apart the jaws of their trap. Her love made her too weak to try.

So the next move was Barrett's. That he possessed the strength to free himself was obvious in the hard length of his body, the steely sinews of his muscles, the harsh tenacity of his restless hands. The power of his body was rivalled only by that of his desire to be free, Caroline knew. How long would it be, she demanded of herself tormentedly, how long . . .?

'I've got to stop this,' she reproved herself. Somehow she had to find the will to go on after Barrett had gone, if only for Stacy's sake. Stacy. Caroline groaned. How would Stacy react when she discovered that Barrett would no longer be a part of their lives? She loved him so much . . . To her, he was a friend and a leader, everything she had always been told a father should be. Would she blame Caroline? To a seven-year-old it would seem so simple. Barrett loved Stacy, so if he left, it had to be Caroline's fault. Could Caroline live with Stacy's resentment on top of everything else? The endless, unanswerable questions chased madly through her confused mind.

Barrett did love Stacy, Caroline reminded herself bracingly. He felt for her all the love and wonder of a natural parent. It was possible that he would stay with Caroline for Stacy's sake. The thought terrified Caroline. She could never carry it off. She would never be able to hide from him all the love that she felt. There was no painless way out for her, no way she would ever be free of the love Barrett so obviously did not want . . .

No sound penetrated her thoughts, but the prickling sensation of being watched tore Caroline's sightless eyes from the window, drawing them unerringly to the doorway of the room. Barrett stood at the entrance, leaning heavily against the door frame, his silver eyes trained on her intently. Even from that distance, he seemed to loom over her, his very size intimidating.

'Barrett!' Caroline breathed weakly, her heart slamming painfully against her breast. 'You frightened me!'

He eased his weight from the doorway, straightening to cross the room to her side, and she sucked in a stricken breath as he neared, and she saw his face. His skin was a sickly white, his nostrils pinched and his eyes narrowed in weak defiance of unending agony. His long, sensual mouth was thin and tight, held in taut control. He looked, Caroline thought, like a man about to snap apart.

'Barrett,' she repeated weakly, 'what's wrong? There's something wrong! Is it Stacy? Has something happened to Stacy?'

'No, Stacy is fine,' he gritted out, the words barely making it past his throat.

'Thank God,' Caroline whispered shakenly. 'What is it, Barrett?' she persisted. 'Tell me why you look like that.'

'How do I look, Caroline?' he enquired tautly, his

eyes fixed on her face with a kind of raw hunger that started tiny shudders of arousal teasing at her pulse.

'You look——' she paused, eyes moving over his stiff face and burning silver eyes, '—as though someone has just given you the most ... beautiful, wonderful present in the world, and told you that if you touch it, it would disappear ...' she trailed off as Barrett's eyes closed on a sharp stab of agony and his big body flinched. 'Barrett?' she questioned in concern.

His lids opened at the sound of his name on her lips, their depths haunted and bruised. 'How apt,' he derided gratingly, 'the most beautiful present in the world!'

'Barrett, please, tell me what's wrong. I can help you——'

'No,' he denied roughly, enigmatically. 'You'll need my help.'

'You're home early,' Caroline probed carefully.

'Yes,' he agreed tensely. 'I had—something to do this afternoon. I came home when I finished. Any objections?' A dark brow shot up in silent challenge.

Yes—a million! Caroline thought achingly. Don't you know that every minute, every second with you is a sweet torment? 'No, no, of course not,' she denied aloud.

Barrett dropped heavily on the seat beside her, running restless fingers through his ruffled hair. A deep tension hung between them.

'I have to talk to you,' Barrett ground out finally, staring blankly at his whitening knuckles as he searched for his next words.

Caroline tensed expectantly. Here it comes, she thought sickly, drowning in the silence. He's trying to find a way to tell me to leave, that he doesn't want me any more. His love for Stacy wasn't enough to keep him after all, she thought sadly. Her own mouth stretched in stiff control, her fiery head bent like that of a criminal awaiting his sentence to be pronounced, she waited for his next words.

'I told you I had something to do this afternoon,'

Barrett reminded her in a dragging voice. Drawing a deep breath, he continued. 'The truth is, I received a phone call. It was from Dr Hilton.' His steely eyes met hers squarely, measuring the shock he read there. 'He asked—to see me.'

Caroline met his eyes blankly, her stunned mind grappling with his words. Dr Hilton? Edward had called Barrett, taken him away from his office to speak with him, and now Barrett was here, wrestling stiffly with words. The two men did not know each other, of that she was sure. The only thing they had in common is me, she determined grimly. The only thing they would have to talk about, me . . .

'My God,' she whispered shakily, her eyes locked on her twisting hands. 'It must have been something more than exhaustion if he felt he had to talk to you . . . Is it serious?' she demanded tightly.

Barrett reached to grasp her hands, gently unknotting them with a fierce concentration that brought a frown to his face, finally smoothing her fingers against his strong palm. Caroline tore her jewel eyes from his hands and studied his face, breath catching in her throat at the gentleness etched in his drawn features.

'Honey, you're pregnant.' His voice was calm and careful, his guarded eyes watchful.

She watched his lips form the words, uncomprehending, speechless.

'Pregnant?' she whispered thickly. 'I—you——' she broke off, her mind whirling chaotically, rendering her incapable of logical speech. Only one clear thought struggled through—the knowledge that she was carrying Barrett's child and that this was something he could not deny her, as he had denied her his love. A fierce tide of gladness clutched at her heart.

Barrett studied her face frustratedly, unable to decipher the emotions chasing unguardedly across her face.

Caroline began to order her confused mind, grasping at thoughts and holding them still for her perusal.

Barrett would not leave them now: she knew this for a certainty. He would stay with them for the child—his child, made without love, but nonetheless formed from his seed. She pictured the long years before her, having Barrett, but not really having him, watching his child grow up and away . . . her eyes became bleak.

This Barrett read easily, and tensed.

'Caroline,' he began starkly, 'I know you don't want this baby . . .'

'Do you want this baby, Barrett?' she asked yearningly.

'That's not an issue any more, is it, Caroline? The baby is a reality. Our child——' he choked slightly as the words seemed to catch in his throat, 'our child will need both a mother and a father——'

'I won't leave, Barrett, not now,' she interrupted flatly.

'I'm sorry——'

'Please!' Caroline waved the apology aside. God, please don't let him think I did this to trap him, she prayed desperately. Please make him love our child a little. 'Don't apologise. Nothing can change what— happened.'

Neither spoke for long minutes.

'If there's anything you want,' Barrett broke the strained silence, 'anything you need . . .'

'I want you,' she whispered huskily, her eyes on the floor.

Barrett did not move. Not by so much as a flicker of an eyelash did he betray any reaction, and Caroline cringed at the thought that she had embarrassed him with her need.

'You want—me?' he repeated finally, his tone strangled.

She nodded, once.

'When?'

The abrupt question startled her. Her eyes met his finally.

'Now,' she whispered. 'Tomorrow. The next night.'

'Why?' The single syllable was rough, driven.

'Because . . . you're my husband. I'm pregnant with your child,' she said reluctantly, then, drawing a deep shuddering breath, continued, '. . . and I—love you.'

Barrett stopped breathing. His long body tensed brittly and his eyes became twin grey walls that defied assault.

'Barrett——?' Caroline prompted, frightened. Would he be angry now, or filled with pity? Embarrassed, or satisfied? It had taken every ounce of courage she possessed to say those three simple words, and she was in agony waiting for his response.

Suddenly he jack-knifed to his feet, standing stiffly beside her, his moves jerky, unco-ordinated.

'Where is Stacy?' he grated hoarsely.

Caroline's shoulders slumped. He was going to ignore it. She had her answer: she had embarrassed him.

'She's going to the Clarks' house after school,' she responded dully. 'I'm supposed to pick her up at six o'clock.'

Barrett crossed to the phone, punching out numbers punishingly. He was silent as he waited for the phone to be answered on the other end, and the silence in the room was smothering.

'Betty?' he bit out unexpectedly, and Caroline jumped. 'This is Barrett . . . I'm fine . . . No, the reason I called was to ask if you could possibly keep Stacy overnight tonight. No, there's nothing wrong. Caroline and I would just like a little time to ourselves.' The bitter laugh that followed struck a discordant note. 'Yes, we're still newlyweds,' he agreed stiffly, obviously to a teasing comment from Betty Clark. 'Thank you. Tell Stacy we'll see her tomorrow. Goodbye.'

He replaced the receiver quietly and turned to face Caroline, his face expressionless. 'They'll keep her the night.'

She nodded, not knowing what to say.

'When you don't want me, tell me,' he ordered harshly. 'I won't force you. Not again.'

Caroline her head, bewildered. 'I want you.'

Barrett crossed the room, coming within inches of her where she remained seated at the window. He dropped to his knees in front of her, raising his hands to cup her face.

'You're sure?' he demanded tautly.

'Yes,' she answered huskily, starving for his touch. Taking the initiative, she leaned forward, pressing her lips to his.

He went rock-still, neither responding nor rejecting as her lips moved enticingly over his own. Finally, a half-muffled groan was ripped from his throat, and his fingers tightened demandingly on her cheeks.

'How long, Caro?' he demanded roughly. 'How long do you want me?'

Until you get tired of me, her heart cried, until you send me away. Her eyes closed tormentedly. 'I don't know,' she breathed. 'Please, don't ask . . .'

Barrett nodded sharply, his mouth white. 'I want you, Caro,' he forced out tightly. 'I want you now.'

'Then take me, Barrett,' she invited explicitly. Rising gracefully to her feet, she held a hand to him, still on his knees before her. 'Take me now, Barrett.'

Her hand in his, Barrett got to his feet, his eyes locked hotly with hers. Together they walked up the stairs to his bedroom.

The months passed quickly, spring changing to summer, summer surrendering to fall. Caroline and Barrett lived in a kind of cautious harmony, opening up to each other on many levels, yet still maintaining a distance, their most intimate thoughts warily hidden.

Since the night Caroline had agreed to stay, she had shared his bed, and he had made love to her tirelessly. But in the passion dark moments, when she lost herself in his arms, some part of Barrett remained aloof, coldly controlled even as he groaned his pleasure and need. Caroline had long since stopped trying to suppress her love, whispering the words feverishly in the darkness of the night as he held her locked in his hungry arms.

Each time she admitted her love, winding her body more closely to his in the night, Barrett would stiffen for one infinitesimal second, a space of time so short that afterwards she would always wonder if she had imagined it, before tightening his hold and taking her once more to the edge of paradise and beyond.

During the first few weeks, she waited eagerly for his response to her admission of love. But Barrett never said a word, never acknowledged her words. Gradually, Caroline accepted that he could not return her feelings, that her love had probably embarrassed him. And still she could not prevent the words from spilling out.

She would have lost him by now, were it not for their baby, she realised sadly. Barrett was exquisitely tender, gently supportive as the months passed. He watched her every move, it seemed, always ready with an encouraging smile or a soothing word when the weight of the baby on her small frame began to make her ungainly and uncomfortable. There were times when she was sure he was wishing he could alleviate her burden somehow, and take on the discomfort that plagued her body as the months passed. She loved him all the more for the helpless, concerned light that haunted his eyes.

He suffered through her cravings for peanut butter, jelly and ketchup sandwiches for breakfast with stoic silence, and ran out at two in the morning for tacos and ice cream without complaint.

One night, well into her seventh month, Caroline was unable to sleep because of the baby's restless movements. At first she simply lay still in the darkness, listening to Barrett's even breathing as he slept beside her, but as the movements continued, she grew restless, tossing and turning beneath the covers. The motion awoke him.

'Honey?' his voice reached out to her soothingly.

'The baby is restless,' she told him wryly. 'I can't sleep.'

His body shifted towards her.

'Come here,' he murmured softly, pulling her gently

against his warmth. His hands roamed lightly over the
swell of her abdomen, absorbing the tremors from the
baby's turns. 'What does it feel like inside?' he asked,
his tone reverent.

'What does it feel like outside?' Caroline smiled.

Barrett was silent for a moment, then he answered
quietly, 'An impatience. A need, I think, unsatisfied.'

She shivered at the description. It hit too close to
home. Her hunger for his love was like that—impatient,
insatiable.

Barrett mistook the cause of her shiver, pulling her
more tightly to his body. 'Does it hurt?' he probed
concernedly.

Caroline shook her head. 'No, not really. It's just—
uncomfortable.'

'Do you want me to rub your stomach?' Barrett
offered gently.

Her eyes squeezed shut. 'That would be nice.'

His hands moved lightly over her abdomen, soothing,
gentle circles that eased the tautness of her muscles,
relaxing her body. He seemed to get as much pleasure
from the action as she did, delighting in the feel of the
restless life beneath his hands.

'Better?'

'Mmm,' she breathed, already half asleep.

'Will you sleep now?'

'If our child will,' she answered wryly.

The touch of Barrett's lips on the rounded swell of
her abdomen snapped her into wakefulness.

'Go to sleep now, baby,' he whispered against her
soft skin. 'Your mommy needs to rest.'

Settling back into the pillows, he once again pulled
Caroline into his arms, her soft, round form moulded to
his hard length.

Caroline, secure and happy in his arms, was asleep in
minutes.

During her ninth month, Barrett's already infrequent
trips to the office ceased altogether. He spent his day

with Caroline and Stacy, taking them on short outings, Caroline carefully bundled up against the winter wind, or stayed home, playing tireless games with Stacy to keep her from wearing Caroline out.

Stacy had received the news of her sister's pregnancy with awe. 'You mean I'm going to have another sister?' she had breathed incredulously when Barrett and Caroline had broken the news.

'Well, not exactly,' Barrett explained easily. 'The baby might be a boy. But whatever sex the baby is, it'll be just like a brother or sister, because you'll live together in the same house. You'll really be the baby's aunt, Stacy.'

'Do you want a boy or a girl, Barrett?' Stacy seized on this point and Caroline had listened with interest. It was a subject that had never come up between them, and she was eager to hear his response.

'It doesn't matter to me, Stacy, not really,' he answered softly. 'I'm going to be the baby's daddy, so it doesn't make any difference whether we have a boy or a girl. All I want is for the baby to be healthy.'

Caroline breathed a silent sigh of relief. She felt the same way.

During the subsequent months, Stacy had watched in awe as Caroline's body filled out, asking her at one point if the baby was going to be round when it made its appearance. Caroline was beginning to wonder, too!

Stacy took her role of aunt-to-be very seriously, insisting that Caroline rest and generally acting like her personal maid, chasing after books that she didn't want and fluffing perfectly fluffy pillows. Caroline took it all in good part, touched by the easy acceptance Stacy showed to the addition to their circle.

One morning in late November, eight days before the baby was due, Caroline woke with a gnawing backache. Shrugging it off, she showered and dressed and began her usual day.

That afternoon, as she sat in the garden, watching as Barrett and Stacy gathered the last of the autumn leaves into a huge pile, the first contraction clenched her body. Caroline drew a sharp breath, her hands resting almost reverently on her abdomen. She remained calm, waiting for the next spasm, timing them mentally.

When they were twenty minutes apart, she raised her eyes to where Barrett and Stacy were playing in the leaves. Barrett was throwing Stacy into the centre of the huge, soft pile, laughing heartily as she climbed out with leaves sticking from odd angles in her hair.

Caroline's eyes became soft and loving. Barrett would be a good, loving father, of that she had no doubt.

'Barrett,' she called softly across the yard.

He turned a smiling face to her, tensing instantly as he registered her pale, set expression. He moved to her, reaching her side in five massive strides. Dropping to his knees beside her chair, he took one of her hands in his, grey eyes concerned as he studied her face.

'Sweetheart? Is something wrong?'

Caroline smiled gently.

'You could say ...' she answered softly. 'The contractions have started.'

All colour drained from Barrett's face, leaving him ashen. His eyes raced to her abdomen, as though looking for visible proof of her words.

'Caro ...'

Caroline never knew what his next words were going to be. Another contraction hit her, this one stronger than the last, and her hand tightened strongly around his. 'Oooh ...'

'Caro!' Barrett took her other hand, offering himself as a release from the pain.

When the pain subsided, she smiled tremulously at his twisted expression. Anyone would think he was in labour! she thought in amusement.

'I think we'd better go to the hospital,' she suggested calmly.

'My God, yes!' Barrett sprang to his feet, running a frenzied hand through his hair. 'We have to drop Stacy off at the Clarks' house,' he muttered, running aloud through their well thought out plans, 'and get your suitcase, and call the doctor——' The words became indistinct as he strode purposefully towards the house.

Caroline eyed his retreating back wryly. Who would have thought Barrett would fall apart in an emergency?

'Can I come, too?' she asked meekly.

He swung around instantly.

'Caro! My God, I'm sorry!' He helped her to her feet with exquisite gentleness, holding her as if she were a delicate piece of china.

Somehow they managed everything, dropping an excited Stacy off at the Clarks' house minutes before they reached the hospital. Caroline did not miss Barrett's relieved sigh as they drew up in front of the building, still in one piece, as it were. She giggled at the insane pun.

Barrett gazed at her in concern, and swept her into his arms, marching into the hospital. Oblivious to the interested stares they drew, he did not stop until he reached the nurse's desk.

'My wife is having a baby,' he informed her sternly.

Caroline giggled again.

The nurse, obviously used to such situations, restrained herself. She calmly called two orderlies to bring a wheelchair, and Caroline was wheeled away to the maternity ward, Barrett closely at her side.

Edward met them there, smiling encouragingly at Caroline as she was taken to the labour room. It took ten minutes of fast talking before he convinced Barrett that he could not go with her. 'Not unless you're in labour, too,' he concluded in amusement.

Barrett rested a hand on his knotted stomach. 'I think I am,' he grimaced.

'Bear up!' Edward advised sympathetically, turning towards the closed doors that led to the delivery room.

Barrett caught his arm urgently as Edward made to pass him, and the doctor turned to him enquiringly.

'We've never talked about this,' Barrett began, his eyes fiercely intent as they met Edward's. 'If anything goes wrong . . . if you have to choose between saving Caro or the baby . . .' he swallowed tightly.

'Barrett!' Edward said calmingly.

'Save Caroline. Whatever you have to sacrifice to do it. Caroline is the most important——'

'Barrett, nothing is going to go wrong,' Edward promised distinctly. 'Caroline is very healthy. I made you a promise that day in my office, and I intend to keep it.'

Barrett nodded, reassured, and Edward left to scrub up, leaving him to pace the waiting room.

He had circled the room exactly six hundred and seventeen times when Edward came out again, pulling the surgical mask from his face and wearily stretching his cramped back.

'Barrett.'

Barrett turned on him instantly, his eyes leaping grey flames. 'It took too long,' he rapped curtly. 'Something's wrong, isn't it?' His tone was at once tormented and savage.

'There's nothing wrong,' Edward assured him happily. 'You have a beautiful baby girl.'

Barrett's eyes softened miraculously. 'A girl,' he repeated thickly, his voice clogged with emotion. 'And Caro?' he demanded urgently.

'—is doing fine. You can see her as soon as we get her to her room. Meanwhile, come and meet your daughter.'

Barrett followed eagerly to the nursery, watching in awe as they placed a tiny baby in a crib marked Rossiter. She was beautiful, he thought dazedly, the most beautiful baby in the world.

'Have you seen her, Barrett?' Caroline asked sleepily, her red-gold hair fanned out thickly against the stiff white hospital sheets.

Barrett was sitting on the side of her bed, his lips moving in soft exploration over every inch of her face.

'Yes,' he whispered against her temple. 'She's

beautiful—pink and cuddly. And she's got your hair,' he finished in smug satisfaction.

Caroline laughed drowsily. 'We must think of a name.'

'We will.'

'And call Stacy . . .'

'I already have,' Barrett soothed. 'You're tired, sweetheart. Go to sleep now.'

'But, Barrett——' Caroline protested weakly.

'I'll be here when you wake up, Caro,' he promised softly, closing her lids with a lingering kiss. 'Sleep now.'

She drifted off to sleep, a happy smile playing on her lips.

Caroline stepped from the steaming stream of the shower, a faint smile tugging at her soft mouth as she began to dry the once again slim contours of her smooth body. It had been over a month since Alexandra Marie had been born, and Caroline had been released from the hospital.

The relationship between Caroline and Barrett had once again undergone a subtle change. A new tension hung between them, an expectant waiting. There were moments when she would catch a haunted, infinitely sad expression colouring Barrett's features before he noticed her attention and drew a blinding shutter closed between them. They did not sleep together. The reasons for this were, at first, obvious. But as the weeks passed, and still Barrett made no move to re-establish their physical relationship, the tension between them increased.

Stacy and Alexandra, with their innocent demands, became a bridge over the chasm yawning between them. Barrett was a doting father, devoting a portion of his day solely to Alexandra and Stacy, somehow balancing his love between the two of them. He had returned to his work at the office, but spent much less time there than he had done before their marriage.

To all intents and purposes, they were a happy, well-adjusted family, but Caroline sorely missed the exchange of confidences and trust that a couple in love would share. Because despite everything, despite Barrett's adoration of their daughter and his continued presence in their lives, he was no closer to loving her than he had been before. Caroline now accepted this resignedly. Maybe it will be enough, she thought hopelessly, maybe it will be enough that he stays.

Shrugging into a silky jade robe that matched her eyes, she left her room to check on the children. After tucking Stacy in, Barrett had disappeared into his study, and Caroline had taken her shower. She doubted if Barrett would appear before she had gone to bed. She sighed. One month of this was a little more than she could stand.

Stacy's room was dark. Caroline stood quietly in the doorway and listened to her sister's even breathing. Out like a light. One down, she thought in satisfaction, one to go.

She crept down the hall, stopping as she reached the faint pool of light cast into the darkened hallway from the nightlight in Alexandra's room. She pushed the door open a little farther, not wanting to disturb the sleeping baby.

Her eyes fixed blankly on the empty bed as she stood in the doorway. It was several seconds before the low, gentle murmur of Barrett's voice penetrated her stunned senses.

He sat in the beautiful old bentwood rocker, Alexandra lying peacefully against his chest, her small, flame hair-covered head tucked securely into his shoulder. She looked ridiculously tiny and fragile against the massive breadth of Barrett's torso. His arms supported her fully, one large hand running soothingly over her pyjama-clad back. So intent was he on the feel of the small body in his arms and on the words he spoke that he did not notice Caroline as she stood in the doorway, her eyes running lovingly over the picture the two of them presented. A small shiver of deep pride and happiness clutched at her throat, and she opened her mouth to speak as Barrett's words to the baby finally registered.

'Allie,' he crooned softly, 'my beautiful Allie. How will you grow up, I wonder, without the loving guidance of a mother?'

Caroline's mouth snapped shut as the words hit her painfully.

'Will you ever be able to understand, to forgive me?' he mused sadly. 'When I found out about you, I was ... ecstatic. The thought that a part of myself would always be bound to a part of Caroline, that the two of us together would live in a child, in you—God, I'll never be able to describe the joy and the wonder that knowledge brought!

'But I knew that Caroline wouldn't be happy. She was going to leave me, you see. Lawrence was dead ... she had Stacy. There was no reason for her to stay. She hadn't fallen in love with me. I tried so hard ... I couldn't let her go.' A sad smile twisted his lips. 'Then suddenly there was you, Allie. And I used you to keep her with me. She promised to stay, honey. She promised to stay for you. But I don't know how long we'll have her, and I——' he admitted brokenly, '—I was afraid to ask. Every day I wake up alone and wonder if this is it, if today is the day she'll leave. And every night I go to bed and thank God that it wasn't. But even that torment of wondering is better than the hell of knowing.'

Caroline's eyes closed in weak defiance of the pain in Barrett's voice. His agony ran as deep and as secretly as her own.

'Your mommy makes me weak, Allie. So damn weak,' Barrett continued achingly. 'She tells me that she loves me, did I tell you that? Every night, as I held her in my arms, she told me she loved me, and I pretended to believe her. Hell, I even got a kick out of hearing it, even knowing it wasn't true. She stays for you, Allie, she says those words for you, but if that's all I can have

. . .' he trailed off, pressing the lightest of kisses to his daughter's temple.

'She's given me so much. How can I ask for more? She gave me you and because of you she gives me herself. But how long can that last? How long until she can't pretend any more?' The soft torment of his tone tore mercilessly at Caroline's heart, and she clenched her teeth to prevent herself from crying out. She had to hear it all. She knew, with a deep sureness, that this was the cause of Barrett's wariness. And she knew that he would never confide in her this way, never bare his soul to her as he was to this child who could not fathom the pain and the fear he admitted to.

'Maybe she won't leave for a while, and we'll have more time with her. You look like your mommy, did you know that?' Barrett continued idly, a gentle finger tracing the baby's sleeping features. 'That's an advantage for us. It would be hard for Caroline to accept a child who looked like me—like a living memory. I forced you on her, you see,' he admitted muffledly. 'God, how bitter she must be to have to accept my child! But you look like her, and having you, having your love, will almost be like having Caro. A little of her—even if it comes through you, Allie—is more than I dared ask for or expect.

'And when she leaves——' he caught his breath with a painful sharpness at the words, '—when she leaves, I'll still have you. It's not that she doesn't love you, Allie. I'll have to make you understand that,' he whispered pleadingly. 'But I know it's hard for her to look at you without—remembering that you are a part of me and that you were conceived . . . It's not your fault, Allie. The blame is mine. I asked too much of her, wanted too much. You must never blame her for leaving us. It's my fault . . . if I could have loved her less, needed less . . .' The words faded tiredly, as though he had gone over and over them and still could not find freedom from their refrain.

'I won't let you forget your mommy, Allie. Every day

I'll tell you about her, about her smile and her flame-coloured hair just like yours, and the sweet smell of her skin and the warm heaven of her arms. I'll give her to you the way she gave you to me . . .'

Barrett held his daughter for long, silent minutes before a deep sigh was issued from his lips. Rising carefully to his feet, he moved to lay Alexandra tenderly in her crib. The baby did not awaken as the warmth of his body was withdrawn. Bending, he placed a light kiss against his daughter's forehead.

'I love you, Allie,' he pledged, straightening as he turned to leave the room.

It was only then that he saw Caroline as she stood silhouetted in the doorway, tears spilling slowly from her glittering green eyes.

Even in the weak light spilling from the nightlight, Caroline saw the way he blanched as he registered her presence.

'Is that what you think?' Caroline's broken voice snapped the taut silence hanging between them, her eyes accusing as they studied Barrett's stiff, closed face.

'Caro . . .' He spoke finally, his voice tight and thick, as though someone had a stranglehold on his throat. 'How—much did you hear?'

Caroline did not answer directly. 'Do you really think I could leave you, leave our daughter?'

'I can't . . . Oh, God, Caroline, I don't want you to go,' he told her tormentedly, 'but I don't know if I could bear to keep you against your will.'

'Ask me . . . you never asked me if I wanted to stay.'

Barrett's hands clenched whitely at his sides. 'Because I already knew the answer.'

Caroline closed the distance between them, her eyes holding his steadily as she stood before him. Her hands fluttered up to rest on the sides of his neck. He flinched briefly, but did not break away.

'I want to stay,' she told him slowly and clearly, as though speaking to a backward child. 'I will never leave you. Never. You're my family now, you and Stacy and

Allie. Do you honestly think I could ever let you go?'

'Why?' the question was torn through fear-whitened lips.

'I love you,' she answered intently. 'I love you.'

'Don't——!' Barrett began sharply, before pulling himself up and continuing in a more level tone. 'Don't say that, Caro. It doesn't matter if you don't love me, just as long as you promise to stay.'

'I love you, Barrett,' she insisted quietly.

'If it's just for Allie——' he began cautiously.

'I love you. I loved you when I gave birth to our daughter. I loved you on our honeymoon. I loved you when I married you. I loved you the night you came to my apartment and saved me from Lawrence,' Caroline enumerated clearly, all pride thrown aside. She had to convince him.

Barrett shook his head. 'It's gratitude, Caroline, because I stopped him, and helped you get Stacy.'

'Gratitude doesn't make me dizzy with hunger for the feel of your lips, the touch of your hands. It doesn't make me forget the world when I'm in your arms,' she denied huskily.

'Caro . . .' he groaned, pulling her into his arms, holding her so tightly she was afraid she would break. 'I'm afraid to believe. I love you so much, from the moment I met your eyes across Ronald Waxler's office, I've loved you. If I accept what you're offering now, I'll never be able to let you go. Can you live with that? Live with a man who can't bear to let you out of his sight for more than ten seconds at a time, live with this constant, insatiable need I have for the touch of your body, the warmth of your smile?'

'I can't live without that, Barrett,' she answered simply. 'But why did you stop making love to me after our honeymoon? Were you really tired of me?'

'Oh, sweetheart, no!' he denied in a smothered tone. 'It was that last night I made love to you,' he explained, a flash of remembered agony tightening his mouth. 'You cried. I was holding you in my arms and you cried, and every tear burned into my heart. I thought that you hated what had just passed between us, that you had to force yourself to ... I thought I had hurt you with my need to make love to you.'

'Barrett, no!' she cried instantly, her hand caressing his face, soothing away the lines of pain that cut into it. 'It was because I was trying to convince myself that I could live without your love——'

'Caroline!'

'—but not without you,' she continued achingly. 'I knew you wanted me. I thought I could love you enough for both of us.'

Barrett's body relaxed perceptibly. 'And I thought the same damn thing when I asked you to marry me,' he confided wryly, his arms tightening lovingly. 'I knew that you thought you needed me to get custody of Stacy. I thought I could love you enough so that it wouldn't matter that you felt nothing for me.'

'And did it matter?' she prompted, her tone half teasing, half agonised.

'Yes!' Barrett hissed. 'Yes, it mattered. There were times when I couldn't—when I wasn't sure if I could go on without your love, times when I didn't want to go on ...'

'We've been so blind,' Caroline condemned sadly.

They stood together in silence, both occupied with the time they had wasted, the hours they had not spent in each other's arms.

But something Barrett had said tugged insistently at Caroline's mind, forcing her out of her reverie. 'Barrett ... what did you mean—I "thought" I needed you to get custody of Stacy?'

'Well, sweetheart ...' Barrett began cautiously.

'Yes?' she prompted, digging an ungentle finger into his ribs.

'There wasn't a court in this country that wouldn't have given you custody of Stacy. All you had to do was to tell someone about his abuse of you, and his drinking, and Stacy would have been yours. I knew it, and Redden knew it,' he concluded grimly, the mention of Lawrence's name bringing back all the furious hatred he felt for the man who had abused Caroline.

'Is that why he signed over custody so easily?' she asked curiously.

'That—and a few threats about a prison sentence,' Barrett admitted reluctantly. He had never told Caroline about Lawrence's offer to sell him Stacy, and he would not now. The man had caused enough pain while he was alive; Barrett would not allow him to inflict any more from his grave.

'You sneaky, devious man,' Caroline said mildly, not in the least bit angered by his deception. 'Tricking a desperate, innocent girl——' she fluttered her long lashes madly, '—into marrying you. Have you no shame?'

Barrett did not laugh back as she expected. 'I was—ashamed on our honeymoon,' he told her hesitantly, his face sombre. 'That first night, when I took your virginity.'

'That first night, when we *made love*,' Caroline corrected quietly, 'was one of the most wonderful, satisfying experiences of my life, Barrett.'

'I hurt you——' he began thickly.

'For one second. And then you brought me hours of ecstasy.'

'I forced Allie on you . . .' he began remorsefully.

'Allie was made with love,' Caroline denied fiercely. 'You never forced anything on me, and certainly not Allie.'

Barrett's mouth softened miraculously, the self-condemnation dying from his eyes. 'God, I wanted to cry in sheer joy when Edward told me about the baby! The thought of my child growing in you . . . We owe him so much, Caro.'

'Yes,' she agreed softly. 'He's been a friend to me all of my life, and he was wonderful to my mother.'

'He loved her, Caroline,' Barrett murmured, watching her closely.

'I know,' she answered softly. 'I finally figured it out

when I went to see him that time. Lawrence must have seen it long ago,' she reflected thoughtfully. 'That must be why he refused to let Edward care for Mother.'

Caroline felt the twisted tautness of his hard body, and looked up at him questioningly. 'Darling?'

'Redden.' Barrett spat out the name bitterly. 'I hate the sound of him! Every time I hear his name . . . I think about the pain he inflicted on you and Stacy. I hate him, Caro. I wanted to kill him for what he did to you, to Stacy . . .' His face was darkly savage as he recalled the cruelties of the man. 'I wanted to kill the bastard for every bruise he put on you . . .'

'Hush, Barrett,' she soothed, alarmed at the tense hatred filling his body and poisoning his mind. 'He's dead. He can never hurt me again. I told Stacy once that he could never really hurt me, and it was true. Only love gives that power, and I didn't love him. I can find it in my heart to be sorry for him now, because he loved my mother so much in the beginning. It was her inability to love him in return that twisted him.'

'That doesn't excuse——' Barrett began explosively.

'Of course it doesn't.' Caroline agreed. 'But he's gone. We can forget him now.'

He relaxed with effort, sighing. 'You're right, sweetheart. We've got better things to talk about.'

'Like how much I love you?' she suggested sweetly, and was rewarded with a long, passionate kiss that threatened to submerge them both in its depths.

'All those nights I held you,' Barrett mused sadly, finally tearing his hungry mouth from hers, 'and listened to you say those words . . .'

'You didn't believe me, did you?' she questioned gently.

'No,' he admitted. 'I thought you were trying to make the best of a bad situation, that you knew you had to stay because of the baby, and you were going to do your damnedest to make it work, even if you had to lie——'

'Except I didn't lie,' Caroline insisted. 'I loved you

then, as I love you now. I never meant to tell you. And when I did, you didn't say a word. I thought I'd embarrassed you,' she recalled painfully.

'Embarrassed me? Caro, if you only knew! The words tortured me. I was afraid one night I'd snap, the way I did that night when I walked in on you in the bath . . .'

'Barrett . . .' She reacted instinctively to the pain in his voice, her fingers feathering across his twisted features.

'I couldn't stop myself from holding you that night, Caro,' he admitted sadly. 'But I paid for it in the long, dark hours of the morning, thinking I'd hurt you again . . . I wanted to beg you to love me, to say the words, even if they weren't true.'

'I love you, Barrett,' she whispered soothingly, pressing her lips to his jaw. 'I've always loved you.' Her lips moved to his chin.

'You're asking for trouble,' he warned unsteadily, as her mouth moved to tease at his.

'I was hoping you'd notice,' she answered complacently, just before his mouth claimed her again.